CONTEMPORARY AMERICAN FICTION

VANISHING ANIMALS

Mary Morris is the author of *Nothing to Declare: Memoirs of a Woman Traveling Alone*, which was cited by *The New York Times* as one of the most notable books of 1988; and two collections of short stories: *Vanishing Animals*, which was awarded the Rome prize by the American Academy and Institute of Arts and Letters, and *The Bus of Dreams*, which won the Friends of American Writers Award. She is also the author of two novels, *Crossroads*, published in 1983, and *The Waiting Room*, published in 1989. She resides with her family in New York City.

Vanishing Animals

& Other Stories

MARY MORRIS

with drawings by Abigail Rorer

PENGUIN BOOKS

PENGUIN BOOKS
Published by the Penguin Group
Viking Penguin, a division of Penguin Books USA Inc.,
375 Hudson Street, New York, New York 10014, U.S.A.
Penguin Books Ltd, 27 Wrights Lane,
London W8 5TZ, England
Penguin Books Australia Ltd, Ringwood,
Victoria, Australia
Penguin Books Canada Ltd, 2801 John Street,
Markham, Ontario, Canada L3R 1B4
Penguin Books (N.Z.) Ltd, 182–190 Wairau Road,
Auckland 10, New Zealand

Penguin Books Ltd, Registered Offices:
Harmondsworth, Middlesex, England

First published in the United States of America by
David R. Godine, Publisher, Inc., 1979
Published in Penguin Books 1991

1 3 5 7 9 10 8 6 4 2

PUBLISHER'S NOTE
These stories are works of fiction. Names, characters, places, and incidents either are the
product of the author's imagination or are used fictitiously, and any resemblance to actual
persons, living or dead, events, or locales is entirely coincidental.

The following stories have been previously published in somewhat different form: "Holland" and "Among the Cuban Refugees" in *The Paris Review*; "Idaho As It Seemed" and "The Other
Moon" in *The Agni Review*; "Foolish Pleasure" in *Triquarterly*.

I would like to thank the National Arts Club, The Bread Loaf
Writers' Conference, and the National Endowment for the Arts
for their support. And a special thanks to Sharon Dunn and
Askold Melnyczuk of *The Agni Review* for their help.

THE LIBRARY OF CONGRESS HAS CATALOGUED THE HARDCOVER AS FOLLOWS:
Morris, Mary, 1947–
Vanishing animals & other stories.
CONTENTS: Holland.—Degree of difficulty.—Charity.
—[etc.]
I. Title.
PZ4.M8782Van   [PS3563.087445]   813'.5'4   79–52637
ISBN 0–87923–286–2 (hc.)
ISBN 0 14 01.5299 7 (pbk.)

Printed in the United States of America

to my parents

Contents

Preface

WHEN I WAS coming home from school one day, I saw a bird, larger than myself, sitting in the lower limbs of a tree not far from our house. As I stopped to look, the bird stretched its wings so that the tips reached to the ends of the limb, which must have been almost ten feet, but I wasn't frightened. I watched it alone for the rest of the day and when my mother came looking for me, she saw it too. Then the zoological society came with cameras and binoculars. The bird had no bands on its legs and wasn't missing from any zoo. The zoological society said we should keep our pets and small children inside and eventually it would fly away. A bald eagle, a thousand miles off course or perhaps simply curious, had flown down from the Rockies to the flatlands of the Midwest. Falling asleep that night, I tried to understand what had brought it so far from where it belonged; I wondered what it would be like, to live where it was craggy, not flat. In the morning I went back to the tree but the eagle was gone.

Several years later I thought I was in love with a boy who sat two rows behind me and one across in study hall. While my friends learned American history and foreign languages, I charted the distance between our chairs, the paths I could take to reach him. We wrote an endless succession of notes to one another and I learned how they could travel, which rows could be trusted, who would turn the notes in to the proctor. I thought that meetings with people were mysterious, wonderful, explosive.

Once the boy asked me to go out with him. The moon was full and we drove west, toward the farmlands. We drove on a road that would take us to the Rocky Mountains if we kept going. The trees and farms were illumined by moonlight and I found we had nothing to say to one another. We tried but it was useless. He was interested in basketball and poker. I only cared about television and gossip, at least as far as talking about things went. It was as if our point together, the common ground where we met, was only in that study hall, in all those notes we scribbled about nothing at all. He put an arm awkwardly around me and we drove in an uncomfortable intimacy. I think it was the first time I felt lonely, really lonely, the way I now know adults can feel. It was then that I thought I saw the eagle again. It was flying back over the fields, flying back to the tree where I'd spotted it so long ago. I could see the bird as I had years before and I saw what I hadn't seen then. In its eyes, amidst all the beauty and triumph, was a terrible solitude that I finally understood comes from having made such a journey.

I've lived in cities where I can't see the stars and in countries where I can barely speak the language; I still think about the eagle and the boy. About our meetings. For years I couldn't understand what kept my parents together. One evening when I was home visiting them, we went for a walk and passed an antique shop. My mother had slipped her arm through my father's and in the window of the store, I could see the reflection of their faces, though they couldn't see me. They were smiling, pointing to an old brass clock that reminded them of somebody else's brass clock, and I watched them as if they were alone. In all the years I'd known them, I'd never seen how happy they were in their own, private way with one another. It finally struck me; how we barely know one another.

Our meetings aren't so explosive or so wonderful as I once thought but they remain infinitely mysterious to me. Sometimes I think I understand, only to find I never understood at all. This is what has kept me coming back to certain places and certain people over and over again.

SAN MIGUEL, MEXICO
9 JULY 1978

The wise man has no need to journey
forth. . . . Voyages are accomplished inwardly,
and the most hazardous ones, needless to
say, are made without moving from the spot.

Henry Miller
The Colossus of Maroussi

Vanishing Animals

Degree of Difficulty

I'D KNOW LAKE MICHIGAN anywhere. It's a broad, blue lake
and on clear days you can see Indiana and Wisconsin from
the bluff where we lived. When I was fifteen, I used to babysit
for two children whose parents belonged to the Highland Park
Swim Club. I never knew why people in Highland Park needed
a swim club when they had a Great Lake in their backyard but
many thought the lake was dirty. This was before it was dirty.
But Mrs. Berger, the mother of the two children, was addicted
to her swim club as much as she was to the track where she
earned my salary. Sometimes she couldn't pay me for two weeks
and swore me to secrecy. We lived on a bluff a hundred feet
above the lake. There was a tree bent back by the wind and I'd
lean against the tree and look across the lake. Most of Illinois
is corn and highways but I had a view that took me halfway to
Canada and my mother swore Rome wasn't much further away.

When I turned sixteen, Mr. Jensen – the blond former halfback
who ran the club and who'd seen me often with Mrs. Berger's
children – offered me a full-time job during my vacation and
Mrs. Berger urged me to take it. I worked the afternoon shift
from two until closing inside a small glass house that members
had to pass before entering the pool area. Half of my job was
to separate families, lovers, and friends. I pushed a buzzer and
women disappeared to the right, toward their locker room
which was painted a dull shade of rose, and men headed to the

left where a blue-grey maze of lockers awaited them. Then they were reunited on the opposite side of my glass house in a small tub of freezing-cold water which purified their feet before they entered the pool.

But the other half of my job, 'check-in,' was considered crucial. There was a large board with the names of all the members printed on it; the board was covered in clear plastic and a red crayon hung at its side. For the first week, Mr. Jensen coached me. 'That's Mr. Mandel and his wife. He's a judo expert. Two guys from the ghetto didn't know what they were messing with when they took him on one night.' Mr. Mandel's shoulders spanned like a two-by-four. I put a red check beside the Mandels but saw that his wife was leaving (Mr. Jensen whispered at me, 'because her mother's gone crazy in a nursing home'), so I erased Mrs. Mandel. 'Doc Williams and three little ones checking in.' A smiling bald man beamed at me, but Mr. Jensen told me, 'His wife just had her fourth caesarian and isn't doing so hot.' Then there was Jennifer Thompson in the white Ford. 'They're separated and never come on the same day.' Mr. Jensen shared with me his private, memorized file on each member and soon I knew them all by what ailed them.

There were two lifeguards. One was the famous Andy Andrews, champion high diver for the high school team. Andy looked like he just left Malibu with his sun-bleached hair and a body which flowed like one continuous muscle. He was often mistaken for Steve McQueen when he got dressed up and went to Chicago.

Every day at six o'clock when the children's swim teams headed for the lockers, Andy made his way up the ten-meter tower. I pulled my chair to the far right so I could watch from the glass house. He warmed up with a jackknife or a swan dive. Then he did a back somersault, usually in tuck position. After that, his real practice began. He stretched, shook his arms and legs like a wet dog. He jumped up and down at the edge of the board as if someone were making him walk the plank. He performed methodically front and back somersaults in pike and tuck position, reverses and inwards, until he was ready for the twisters. For Andy, the twisters were his most difficult dives and before each dive, he puffed up his face four or five times. Then he dove and, for a moment, it seemed as if he were suspended in mid-air. But soon he was moving through that mysterious series of involuted turns, impossible to really follow, which I could only liken to the DNA model on my science teacher's desk.

The other lifeguard was Scott Rafferty. He was in charge of the pool and was a thin, fragile looking boy with drooping shoulders and long, sapling-like legs. I never knew how he got to be a lifeguard and wasn't sure he could save anyone. When he blew his whistle to discourage teenage boys from trying to drown one another, they laughed behind his back. I could see this from the glass house. Scott owned a car, Andy didn't. I always tried to stall, hoping Andy would invite me to Mac-Donalds, but in the end I got a lift with Scott. When it got dark, Scott checked the gates and Andy folded the deck chairs. I waited at the edge of the pool.

The first night Scott drove me, our conversation centered on Andy. 'You think he's good, don't you?'

Scott nodded but kept his eyes on the road. He said he thought Andy was Olympic material. 'And if he doesn't make the Olympics, I guess he wants to go work for the phone company as a lineman.' I thought that sounded very exciting, to be high above the earth on a telephone pole. Scott seemed restless. He wrapped his fingers tightly around the wheel and let them keep time to whatever was on the radio.

'Are you going to go to college?' Scott was in a five-year medical program in obstetrics at the University of Illinois and he thought college was important.

'Oh, I don't know, I guess so.' I yawned, stared out the window, watching other people's houses go by. He had worked with Andy for three years and I wanted to know more.

'Has Andy tried out for the Olympics yet?'

Scott nodded. 'What are you going to study?' We weren't far from my house now.

'Dental hygiene.' Scott nodded again, this time in approval, but I was lying. I didn't care what I was going to study. That spring my mother had taken my brother and me on a whirlwind tour of every woman's institution from Boston to New York. In New York my brother and I, he was eleven at the time, got lost in the Easter Parade. Actually, our mother lost us when she ambled on to the avenue for a better view. She was wearing a red hat but so were a thousand other women. That's all I remember about going East to look for colleges. My mother's disappearance among the red hats of the Easter Parade.

After I'd been working almost three weeks, Mrs. Berger leaned close to me over the counter as if we were intimates. She tapped her fingers on the side of my glass house and whispered, 'I see they aren't letting you out either, Barbs.' Then she glanced down at her daughters, Sandy and Anna, who clung to her right arm and left leg, respectively. Mr. Jensen was patrolling the pool. 'Is he being nice to you? He's not flirting, is he?' she asked. Illinois can be a secluded place. I knew my science teacher liked me better than anyone else because when my ink-distilling experiment exploded, he let me do it over. But I didn't know how an older man could flirt with me and I'm not sure I knew what the word really meant anyway.

'No,' I said, trying to look stern, 'Mr. Jensen doesn't do that with anyone.'

Mrs. Berger was a dark, voluptuous woman in her early thirties with hair that rose like wild birds. Her husband, a plastics engineer, was excruciatingly patient and spoke like a record being played too slowly. But she always seemed frantic to me. I knew I'd be a terrible mother. Once I brushed Anna's teeth with first-aid cream, mistaking it for toothpaste. I felt especially bad because Anna had a speech impediment which made her call me 'Bawa.' Suddenly Mrs. Berger pulled a wad of money from her beach bag. 'Look.' We bent our heads together, conspiring. 'I won the daily double.' She handed me a two-dollar bill. 'Spend it when you find someone to love,' she said and headed to the locker room.

Andy jumped across the tub of cold water and stood at the

side of my house which faced the pool. 'How was I?' He was dripping wet. I didn't know he'd been diving.

'You were great!' I said. He told me that the next night his father was giving him the car.

We drove up Illinois 295, heading towards Libertyville. A half-moon shone over the cornfields and a skinny scarecrow waved in the wind. His father was a chicken farmer and there were feathers all over the seat. We talked about diving. 'You know, there was Murphy Walker. He made it big and then became coach at Notre Dame when he was thirty-two. He didn't start diving until he was seventeen. Or Bobby Victor. He did a lot of the diving and swimming in the Tarzan movies.' Andy had the future all mapped out. He would make some kind of showing in the '64 Olympics and that would bring him interesting positions in the world. If he didn't make the Olympics, he would work for the telephone company, the way Scott had said. In fact, fifteen years later my mother would write how that kid who used to dive had been sent over by the phone company to repair a line after a storm.

We drove to MacDonalds off Deerfield Road. As we turned into the parking lot, I saw Scott's Dodge, parked over in the shadows. I was suddenly struck with an enormous fear, that he was there with another woman. And for some reason, my own fear frightened me. It took me a moment to see that this car was blue, not grey, and to remember that Scott would never take the route we had taken. I thought how Scott looked when I told him I was driving with Andy that night. He snapped his fingers and clapped his palm on his fist in an alternating rhythm, the way he always did. 'Sure, see you tomorrow.'

We drove again with double cheeseburgers and strawberry shakes in boxes between our thighs. When we finished eating, Andy slipped his arm across my shoulder and headed toward the lake. We parked and he pulled me closer. He kissed me on the cheek and once, briefly, on the lips before I asked him to take me home.

For the next two nights, Scott didn't offer to drive me. I would call my father who drove up and honked. In the car home, he asked questions about how many people had been in the pool that day and did I swim. He wanted to know how many nose-plugs we'd sold. Then he would say how whatever mother had cooked for dinner tasted 'like your foot's asleep,' his expression for all her cooking and most films. When I drove with my father, I missed Scott. Scott asked questions the way my science teacher did. In fact, he never asked one question but a whole series. He wanted to know why I did things. He asked how I was born, which I told him in detail since he was devoting his life to this event. 'I was standing up in the womb like the Statue of Liberty,' I said. 'They had to yank me out.'

'Can I have a ride?' Scott had just come into the office to see Mr. Jensen about a new filter. He cleared his throat and said he wanted to get home right after work. 'It only takes a minute,' I said.

Frances, who ran the hamburger stand, sat with me during my break. She wore a candy-striped uniform which she pointed to. 'Like a hospital,' she said. Frances knew that every member had a mental disorder, an invisible disease, a secret history. What was gossip to Mr. Jensen was clinical to her. 'Now there's the most insecure person I've ever met.' Scott followed the edge of the pool like a soldier in enemy territory. 'He's always snapping his fingers.' Frances shook her head back and forth. 'And he always says "ten-four" when you ask him to do something. And he never talks to girls.'

'He's not a flirt,' I said, the meaning of the word suddenly brought home to me.

I expected him to drop me right off but when we got to my driveway, Scott drove on to the end of the street where the bluff is. We got out of the car and walked along the Indian trail. He went right to my tree, bent back in the wind, even though he'd never been there before. 'You know,' I began hesitantly, 'I'm not really planning to study dental hygiene.' I was afraid he'd never speak to me again. He took a deep breath. 'I didn't think so,' he said. He began picking out constellations. Orion had three stars to his belt. I followed his finger from Orion's belt to the North Star. The finger moved like a hand against a blackboard, sketching a dipper, and I had an enormous desire to take his hand and press it to my face.

Scott was hungry so we went into the kitchen where my mother gave us milk and a Sara Lee coffee cake. The Sara Lee plant wasn't far from our house. Once a week my mother drove to their reject store behind the factory where we purchased upside-down cheese cakes, pies without crusts. This coffee cake had pecans on one half and frosting on the other. It was also flat. Scott stared at the cake.

'We like them this way,' my mother said. Then she added, 'I certainly appreciate your bringing Barbara home like this.'

She left us alone. I had collected rocks from the bluff which I labeled and I brought down some of my collection. He petted my dog and remarked that he never knew there were so many kinds of granite. He had a dog, Nero, who recently ran through the screen door. When Scott left, the screen door banged behind him and I wondered if it hurt to go through a screen door.

A few minutes after I'd crawled in bed, my mother came up from the basement. She pushed my feet aside and sat at the edge of the bed. 'Nice boy, but I thought you liked the blond one.'

'I do. Scott is just a friend.' She nodded slowly. My mother was no fool. When she was fourteen, she took herself down the block to see Isabel, the red-headed stripper, who explained to her the facts of life in about twenty minutes time. The remaining years of her youth were spent fleeing the Midwest and its provincialism, one of Isabel's primary suggestions, until after six engagements in four states, the last one broken by a suicide, my mother took a prop plane through a Nebraska tornado back to my grandmother, who greeted her at Meigs Field after all those years with 'I told you so.' She met my father eight years later when he came into Saks to return a nightgown for his sister and my mother was selling lingerie. 'I took one look at him,' my mother told me once, 'and I knew.' From time to time she admitted she may have been mistaken. 'Well, I've never seen the other one,' she said, 'but Scott has kind eyes.' In the dim light, she looked tired to me. Often late at night, I heard her pacing the house. In the morning, even if I left before seven, the coffee was always brewed.

'Do you know any dives, Ma?'

'Only Angelino's, sweetheart.' She ruffled my hair and turned out the light. Angelino's was a pizzeria in the next town.

When I got to work, Mr. Jensen told me I hadn't erased Mrs. Whitcomb and her children in three days and that I hadn't put Mr. Andrews in for a day and a half. I protested that Mrs. Whitcomb was always there and that Mr. Andrews would crawl down low and slip past me. 'It doesn't matter what the causes are,' Mr. Jensen said, 'you're getting sloppy.'

That night we drove to the end of the street, got out of the car and walked on the Indian trail. Scott leaned his back against my tree and took several deep breaths. 'Think I'll dive from here.' He made a swishing motion with his arms.

'You'll break your neck,' I said. 'There's a sand bar.' Then he pulled me to him, pressed my back against the tree and kissed me on top of the bluff with the lake crashing a hundred feet below and the wind rushing down from Canada.

Sometime after the bombing of Pearl Harbor but before I was born, my father and his brother were on a train. They were architects, going to Meridian to build a store. As the bleak Midwestern landscape rushed by, they started talking about how much easier it would be in the rural districts if you put all the stores in one place. By the time the train reached Mississippi, the first shopping center had been designed.

My father was working at his desk when I told him that the lifeguard who ran the pool and was going to be a pediatrician had invited me to his house in Waukegan. For some reason I couldn't tell my father that Scott was going to be an obstetrician. My father didn't seem to find it remarkable that I was spending the day with a man who was in college but his eyes lit up when he heard Waukegan. "We built the Sunrise Mall there."

The Sunrise Mall had little to do with sunrise, except for the large sunburst Aztec clock on the side of Zayre's which seemed to contradict the rest of the stark structure. We drove past quickly because Scott knew the mall well. He'd told my father that his father had worked for the steel contractor on that job. He and my father had hit it off right away. We came to a row of white frame houses and pulled into one of the steep driveways. When we reached the garage, Scott turned off the ignition. 'I guess I'd better explain some things.' He sighed and stared straight ahead. 'I know things like this aren't supposed to happen but my brother was killed a few years back in a car accident and my father died a month later. From grief, I think. I sort of take care of my mother. You know, she worries a lot.' Then his voice trailed off and he said no more.

A small, dark-haired woman sat on the porch swing. She waved as we walked toward her and kissed both of us. The house was old and smelled like the oil my grandmother put on her hair. Scott prepared the barbecue while his mother gave me the tour. I saw Scott's room with its 'Fighting Illini' banner, its thick medical dictionaries, a plastic skeletal model with all the muscles and veins visible, and the ancient four-poster with a cowboy-and-Indian spread. After the tour, we went to work on the fruit bowl. It was a watermelon, carved like a sailing ship, with a cargo of melon balls which she must have spent hours on. Together we glazed the base in sherbet to resemble the open sea.

Scott had fallen asleep on the porch swing. I sat down beside him and he dropped his hand on my leg. 'Fruit bowl done?' he mumbled. I touched his brow. 'I don't think I've had more than four hours sleep a night since I met you,' he said. 'It'll be good practice for my internship in six years.' He smiled and without opening his eyes pulled me to him and kissed me. As he held me, I saw his mother, watching us from the kitchen window.

After the barbecued spareribs, his mother gave us 'wash-and-dries' and took out the picture album which she'd been hiding on her side of the picnic table. Ignoring Scott's protests, she motioned for me to sit beside her. I saw Scott in her arms; I couldn't imagine him being so tiny. There were pictures of other family members she passed over without explanation. Then pictures from journeys. The Grand Canyon. A house they'd owned in Colorado. The sun seemed to shine out of these pictures. 'That's my lamb.' She pointed to a picture of herself holding a lamb. 'I delivered the poor thing myself, by caesarian section.' Pictures of the state capitol. A brass head of Lincoln, his log cabin, the store in Salem where he worked, Scott in the stocks with a sign which read 'for pillaging.' There were postcards with pictures of Lincoln and captions she had written herself: Honest Abe, Young Rail Splitter, Abe wins spelling bee, Abe reading by kerosene lantern, Campaigning in Peoria, Walking four miles in blizzard to return three cents to a customer. 'He freed the slaves.' His mother pointed an emphatic finger at the album. 'And he came from right here. From Illinois.' Scott was beginning to fidget in his chair and he asked if we couldn't have dessert. 'And he was a writer,' her finger came down again. 'A beautiful writer.' Then she cleared her throat and began reciting the Gettysburg Address. She paused for a moment at the line about a 'great civil war' and I thought she would stop but she went all the way to 'shall not perish from the earth,' after which she proudly brought out her fruit bowl.

'She'll never let him go,' my mother said when I got home. A thin light had shone from beneath the basement door. That was where she worked at night. She sat on the stool in a dirty yellow bathrobe which was opened to her thighs. A Pall Mall hung from her lips and in her hand was a brush and palette. She was painting a woman whose face was turquoise on one side and black like the moon on the other. The woman wore a bonnet. It was the only time I ever saw her painting. 'Mothers like that don't know how to let go.' The strange, adult world often eluded me. I didn't know what a mother had to let go of.

'Is that hard?' I asked.

'What?' She looked at me hazily, then saw I was pointing to the painting. 'Oh, nothing's hard if you put your mind to it.'

I woke at six the next morning to the sound of the lawn mower. From the window, I saw my father cutting the grass. This wasn't unusual, except that it was barely daybreak and my brother had mowed it the day before. I went downstairs and found my mother sitting on the couch in the den. 'Is he crazy?' She shook her head. A cup of coffee teetered on the arm of the sofa. 'He's upset because you stayed out late.' I offered to come home earlier but she shook her head. 'He'll just have to get used to it.' I sat down and together we watched my father shear the lawn like a sheep.

That morning, Mr. Jensen held the first meeting of the Eighth Annual Highland Park Swim Club Mock Olympics, which he abbreviated to Swim-Olym. Andy would do exhibition diving. Scott was in charge of races. Frances and I were supposed to train the Penguins, the girls' water ballet team, to swim in time to 'Moon River' and 'I Left My Heart in San Francisco.' Frances sat in a corner, doodling costumes, while I tried to teach fifteen little girls how to move like swans. Mr. Jensen's little towhead daughter sank. Sandy Berger kept yelling at her, which didn't help. Anna yelled at me every minute, 'Bawa, dis wight?' The Mandels' daughter hated Sandy for some reason and Irv Thompson's daughter, the only one who could really float and scull, was obese and looked like a land turtle. Scott had set up a booth where he took down registrations for the races. I went to Mr. Jensen, 'I wasn't hired for coaching,' I complained, but he wouldn't listen to me.

'I Left My Heart in San Francisco' was scratched. On my break, I borrowed Scott's car and drove to Mr. Michner's store. I used to love to go to his store on Central Avenue because his son, Mark, gave me my first kiss as we danced in the dark to 'Small World.' I would go there after school, pretending to need a book or a record but always hoping Mark would show up. Whenever he did, if I was there, he'd say, 'You here again?' After a while I went because I liked the books and music and because it was a good break on the two-mile hike from school. Mr. Michner didn't have Tony Bennett but said that Andy Williams was just as good. No one would know the difference. I paid for it. 'Mark's been asking about you,' Mr. Michner said as he handed me the package. I nodded but a book on the counter caught my eye. It was a thin book, filled with colored pictures. Starved Rock, Salem, Lincoln's tomb – a new pictorial history of Illinois. 'Hot off the press,' Mr. Michner said. 'It's $2.50.' I opened to the historic section. There were old etchings of Lewis and Clark, the first settlers at Port Clinton, Chief Sitting Bull cross-legged in his jail cell at Fort Sheridan where he died, five minutes from my house.

I reached into my wallet but the only money I had left was the two-dollar bill Mrs. Berger had given me after the daily double. I held it in my hand hesitantly as Mr. Michner reached for it. 'Call it even,' he said. He put the book in a bag, along with a map and some travel brochures.

Even though the days were getting shorter, we were closing later and later. While Scott trained any swimmer who wanted his help, I sat poolside, poring over the pictorial history of Illinois. Abraham Lincoln was ugly and skinny, somewhat like Scott it seemed. I learned how he read by a candle every night. Scott sat down beside me one afternoon while I was looking at the brochures. We let our knees press together over the intimate shots of Mary Todd's dressing room. 'Maybe we could drive down to Salem together,' Scott said. 'I mean at the end of the summer. You could come and interview at Illinois.'

That filled me with readiness for a journey. While working with the Penguins, I led a secret life, something I'd never done before. I saw Scott and me driving on long stretches of highway. Visting Starved Rock, where the Indians had chosen to starve rather than surrender. While Scott was preoccupied with whether women's freestyle should follow men's butterfly or if there should be a separate teenage category, I planned how to ask my parents if we could drive downstate. Every night we stayed later and later and Scott would drop me off sooner. I found that I really didn't care much about how the Penguins did and the less I cared, the more Scott was engrossed in his races.

'Patience is a virtue,' Andy said one evening as I sat in a chair, waiting. I nodded. 'I'm glad you guys hit it off. Hope you live happily ever after.'

That night we didn't leave until after ten-thirty. We were the only ones left and together we folded deck chairs, picked up discarded towels, a lone forgotten sandal, empty tubes of suntan lotion. We checked the gates and made our way to the door. As we opened the door, Scott stopped dead in his tracks. Then he turned and stared at the diving board. He was trembling. 'Did you hear that?' I shook my head. I hadn't heard a sound. 'You know,' he said, 'sometimes when I'm locking up and everyone's gone except you, I think I hear the diving board snap as if Andy were still diving.'

I slipped my arm through his. 'Maybe it's like when you've been at sea for a long time.' Once my father had taken us deep-sea fishing for two days. 'Later, when you sleep on the land, you still feel the boat rocking.'

He shook his head. 'I hear the whole thing. The board spring, the snap, the entry.'

Even though it was very late, Scott insisted we drive to my spot. We got out of the car and went to the tree. 'Maybe you're Superman,' I said.

'Why, 'cause I hear things? Naw. Superman wouldn't live in Waukegan. He'd live in a big house in Lake Forest.'

I started to laugh but suddenly Scott grabbed me. He turned me and pinned me to the tree so tightly I could feel the knotholes against my spine. He wasn't anyone I knew. In a moment he was pressed firmly against me and was saying the word 'please' over and over again in a deep, rasping voice. He wanted something, something terrible it seemed, and, not knowing what it was, I stood motionless against the tree, staring at the sky. Then he stopped, as abruptly as he'd begun, and pulled away. 'You'd better get some sleep,' he said. He walked back to his car. I walked on toward my driveway, watching Scott drive off toward the intersection where, years ago, in our wild days, my brother and I had stolen all the stop signs.

Mr. Jensen's little girl got a cramp in the middle of 'Moon River' and had to leave the pool. After that our performance fell apart. No one could keep time. It was as if we'd never rehearsed. Anna rushed up to me after the show, 'I'm thowwy, Bawa.' She cried on my white slacks. Mr. Jensen blamed it on Andy Williams. 'Last year it was fine with Tony Bennett.'

I mumbled an apology and went off through the crowd. All the members and their families and friends were at the Swim-Olym, dressed in cool pastels and golf shirts. Frances was sulking by the hamburger stand because they wouldn't let her drink beer. Anna clung to me as I made my way through the crowd. I was grabbed from behind. 'Well, look who's here.' Mark Michner shoved a Coke into my hand and patted me on the cheek. 'You've been busy this summer, I guess.' He introduced me to a group of his friends from Winnetka as 'our local historian.' It was true that in the past month I had purchased *Archaeological Sights in Western Illinois, By Thy Prairies Gently Flowing, Mrs. O'Leary's Cow,* the collected Carl Sandburg, and a slightly off-color novel entitled *Soy Boy.* A year ago I would have done anything to have Mark Michner introduce me to a group of his friends but now, when it was actually happening, I found I couldn't have cared less. I made my excuses, saying I had business to attend to. The boys made low whistling noises, wondering what business a high school junior could possibly have to take care of.

I wandered beneath the Japanese lanterns and mosquito bombs to find Scott, who was master of ceremonies. The men's races were finishing and they were the last event before diving. The women's locker room was now officially closed, except for the lavatory area, but, just as Scott was about to make his announcements, I saw two people wander into the locker room. I looked for Mr. Jensen to tell him that two kids had gone into the locker, probably to smoke cigarettes, but I couldn't find him. Andy was making his way up the ten-meter tower and a hush came over the crowd. Scott spoke over the loudspeaker and his voice came from everywhere. He gave a brief biographical history of Andy's career, talked about diving and said how beautiful it was, while Andy finished his warm-ups. Then Andy signaled Scott and the real diving began. 'Now folks, we're going to start with a relatively easy dive for Andy.' Scott announced a front 3½ pike with a degree of difficulty of 2.9. 'It took Andy only two months to perfect this dive. That's quite unusual.' Scott paused as Andy dove. There was a breathless silence. Then Scott announced the next one. Once or twice he glanced over at me and smiled.

Whoever had gone into the locker room didn't come out and I'd been given strict orders. I walked around the pool but Mr. Jensen wasn't anywhere. I sent Anna off to find her parents and headed toward the locker room myself. The door was slightly ajar and I pushed it forward. It opened silently and in the dim light I saw a man and a woman. The woman was slumped forward, almost swooning, and the man was either trying to help or to hold her. As my eyes adjusted to the light, I saw that it was Mr. Jensen and Mrs. Berger. I thought of asking them if they needed any help but for some reason I couldn't bring myself to say a word. I just slipped backwards, opened the door with the back of my hand and left without being seen.

I went into the glass house and opened the windows to watch the rest of the diving. The twisters that were to me a double-helix molecule were coming up and I watched as Andy slowly prepared for them. While he paused for a moment, I picked up the cloth and erased the plastic board for the last time, erased everyone. With the crayon I drew a bird on the board, a migrating bird to mark the end of the season. When I turned, Mr. Berger was standing at the counter. 'Hiya, toots. Seen Mrs. B? I wanta get the kids home.'

'Sorry, Mr. Berger. I haven't. I'll check the locker room for you.' It amazed me, how many lies I'd told since I turned sixteen.

'Nice bird.' He pointed to the plastic board and went away. I walked out of the office and toward the locker area. I pounded on the door, waited a minute, then went in.

'Mrs. Berger,' I shouted. 'Are you here?'

A few minutes later she came out of the shadows. 'I'm not feeling so hot, Barbs.'

She looked old and ugly, a drunken mess. 'You missed the diving,' was all I could say.

Mr. Jensen was sitting in the glass house when I returned. He was erasing the bird. 'You shoulda stuck with Tony Bennett.'

I apologized again. 'Oh, it's O.K.,' and he handed me my last paycheck of the season.

It was well after two A.M. when Scott and I left. 'Wasn't that fantastic, wasn't it great!' he kept saying.

'It was all right. Actually I was kind of bored.'

'Bored. How could you be bored? Everything was great, except for the Penguins.'

I felt my stomach tighten. When we got to my house, he didn't drive to the end of the street. When I asked if he wouldn't drive down, just for a few minutes, he shook his head. 'I promised Mr. Jensen I'd be back to clean up tomorrow.'

'Why don't you stay in our spare room? We can both go in tomorrow.'

He shook his head. 'I told my mother I'd be back.'

'O.K. Well, when will I see you?'

He cleared his throat and pressed his fingers against the steering wheel. 'I've got a lot to take care of this week.'

'We could go to a show tomorrow since you'll be nearby or else I can take the train down during the week and help you pack.' He kept his eyes fixed on the steering wheel and repeated softly that he had a lot to take care of. 'We're still driving to Salem, aren't we?' He was silent and I was like a mad woman. The first time you are in love, everything is new.

He stared straight ahead at the steering wheel which he still clasped, his hands turned inward, fingers on top and grooved around the notches as if he were prying it open. He examined the roundness of the wheel, the scalloped notches, the Dodge emblem in the middle, the horn and the plastic rim around the horn. He touched all its parts, probed and considered, then he put his hands back on the wheel and tried to pull it apart again and, for the first time, he was a doctor, learning the inner workings of a woman.

Something inside of me snapped. I started shouting. 'Just because your father and your brother died and your mother isn't quite all right doesn't mean you can't care about anybody.'

I felt as if I would explode as he looked at me and gasped. 'I mean, it was convenient for you, wasn't it? It was easy. To have me all summer and then just forget about it and go back to school. An easy summer romance.'

I think he said it wasn't easy and that it wasn't a summer romance. If he said that, he was lying.

'It was your idea. I didn't ask for this. I didn't want to be driven home every night. You can't just walk away. I mean, it's not normal.'

'Christ.' Now he was shouting back. 'You're only sixteen. What do you want me to do? Marry you?'

'All right, have it your way.' I reached into my purse and handed him the pictorial history of Illinois with a ribbon around it. 'This is for your mother.' He wouldn't take it so I put it on the seat between us. 'Have it your way. But I can forget you too. I can erase you from my mind in a snap.' I snapped my fingers together to show him how quickly I'd forget. Scott sat beside me silent now. I touched him on the arm. 'Look, I'm sorry.' He didn't move. 'Boy, are you a phony,' I opened the door, my voice beginning to break. 'You're about as phony as . . .' For a moment I couldn't think of anything to match his phoniness. 'As a three-dollar bill.'

I was out of the car and slamming the door shut, heading up the stone path, before I knew what had happened. I reached our front door, which was always left ajar for me, but, as I opened it, I heard another car door slam. Scott was rushing toward me with his arms extended. He grabbed me and held me in his arms. He kissed me as he'd first kissed me on the bluff and I held him, ready to give whatever it was he wanted. But then, suddenly again, he was gone. He raced into his car and zoomed out of the driveway. His headlights were disappearing as I raced to the intersection where we'd stolen the stop signs and called to him, my arms outstretched, clutching the pictorial history of Illinois which he'd thrust back into my hands as he dashed for the car.

The next morning, just after seven, my father came outside

to see what I was doing. He paced back and forth on the brick path. 'Are you all right?' he called to me impatiently. 'What the hell are you trying to do?' he shouted. Then he just shook his head at me. My father sat down on the brick wall of the patio, with a cup of coffee and the *Tribune* in his hand, and he watched me mow the lawn.

Charity

LILLIAN JACKSON CAME to us from Meridian, Mississippi, along with her son, Arthur, who was six at the time, my brother's age. We went to meet them at Union Station and before she was even introduced, she swept down on me and I disappeared into the folds of her flesh which tumbled over me like the sea. Arthur stood back, occasionally peering from behind his mother where he had successfully hidden himself, and from time to time his big dark eyes would stare at my brother, David. Lillian had to do a fast spin to pry the shy, retiring boy loose and get him to say hello. She called me 'child' and David 'boy.' 'Well, child,' she said to me, 'I can see you're smart like your Mama said and we's gonna have a good time.' And to David, 'I can see you's about as good as any little boy can be.'

My father treated Lillian as he would treat any woman. He took her bags and led her by the arm. My mother took David in one hand and Arthur in the other. Arthur looked so frightened of my mother that I was certain no white person had ever touched him before. Lillian clutched my hand and we all walked out of the station. 'Um hum,' Lillian said, almost with a moan, 'I ain't never seen anything so tall.' We were outside now and she was referring to the city of Chicago.

'We don't live in the city,' my father said, trying to make her more at ease.

'We live in a house in the country,' my mother added. And Lillian said she was sure it would be just fine.

Before Arthur and Lillian came to us, my mother explained that she had found out about Lillian through an agency that assisted poor blacks who lived in the South. The agency found them work and placed them with responsible families who agreed to sponsor them for one year. When my father started making decent money, they had done the same with German girls who wanted to leave Germany just after the Second World War. My parents thought that having German girls in the house would keep us open-minded and not hate all Germans for what 'one lunatic had done.' The German girls smelled as if they bathed in disinfectant and they ate food which smelled so bad it made my father double over and grimace as if he had actually eaten something he didn't like. I learned words from them like 'gut nacht' and 'was is das?' and I taught them 'nudnik' and 'kvetch.' Finally one of the girls started 'blowing up like a balloon,' as my father put it, and my mother said maybe we should try something different. 'We don't need that going on around here,' she said to him over breakfast one Sunday. Thus Lillian.

Lillian waddled up and down the stairs in her big blue skirts and the whole house shook when she laughed. She was her own private earthquake, it seemed. When she wasn't laughing she was singing, and neither seemed to upset the even, though ponderous, rhythm of her bed changing or dish washing. At breakfast, when she handed my father his toast with 'Nobody Knows the Trouble I've Seen' or his eggs with 'Sweet Chariot,' my father said, 'So how's Mahalia Jackson The Second today?'

Lillian and Arthur slept curled up together in the same bed, arms and legs wrapped around one another. They even breathed in unison. I know because one night I woke up, feeling ill, and, for some reason, instead of waking my mother, I went into Lillian's room. I stood at the foot of the bed, watching them sleep interlaced, their chests rising and falling together. After a while Lillian opened her eyes and for a moment she looked at me oddly as if she thought she was seeing an angel. Then she said, 'What's wrong with you, child?' I don't remember what was wrong but I remember that I crawled in with them and the three of us lay curled in that bed, Arthur with his arms and feet now wrapped around me, my hands around his, Lillian enveloping both of us, in that room that smelled like a bear's cave. In the morning I overheard my mother saying to Lillian in the kitchen, 'I don't care if you didn't want to bother us; next time it happens, bring her to me.'

They came to us in the Year of the Chicken. The Year of the Tuna had just ended and my father had breathed a sigh of relief. I had a childhood syndrome in which I only ate one kind of food for the better part of a year and my father likened my periods of devotion to the Chinese calendar. It was obviously an obsession, a need for consistency which I'm sure had very complex roots. My parents used to stand over my lunch, wringing their hands, books on malnutrition lying open on the table.

To everyone's awe and amazement – the nutritionists my parents had consulted, the family doctor, all my relatives – Lillian got me to eat green vegetables in spite of the fact that my mother had warned her with a sigh, 'She won't eat anything but chicken.'

To which Lillian had replied, 'I bet she'll eat some nice creamed spinach if I make it just for her.' And so for five days she made creamed spinach and on the sixth, without fanfare, I forgot my obsession and ate it. Given Lillian's other quirks, she would not have lasted as long as she did if it had not been for the miraculous effect she had on my eating habits. Looking back, I'm sure she got me to eat normally because she never made any fuss about it. She just put the food on my plate and if I didn't touch it threw it away without a word. But to everyone she had achieved the impossible and so, for a time, my parents tolerated the ghosts and the irrevocable bond which was soon welded between Arthur and David.

Of all the ghosts, and there were hundreds, at least one in every inanimate object, Lillian attached the greatest importance to only two. The first was that of my paternal grandmother who lived in the upstairs cedar closet where my mother had carefully packed away her things when she died. Whenever Lillian was told to get something down from the closet, she made me come along. 'You know her better than I do,' she used to say. If anything went wrong and we somehow upset Grandma's ghost, I was to do the explaining. My mother had great difficulty accepting Lillian's belief that my father's mother's spirit dwelled among the purple boas and velvet capes. But when something had to be retrieved from storage, Lillian always took me by the hand, saying 'Innocence keeps the demon away.'

The other ghost, though it was never clear to me if it was actually a ghost or some cursed memory we were dealing with, was Arthur's father, Abel. Abel, it seemed, could do anything. He slammed doors, made children fall down, and burned toast. If the cat knocked over the milk bottles, Abel had gotten the cat to do it so that 'these poor children won't have milk before they go to school.' Abel was also the great castigator. 'Now Abel,' Lillian would say, staring into empty space, 'what do we do with a boy who won't share his train with his sister?' And sometimes, if things went very bad, Lillian's eyes would tear and she would shout, 'Abel, it's all your fault. You did this to us, you made it happen. If it weren't for you, we wouldn't be in this mess in the first place. You're bad and you got no mercy in your heart.' When she spoke this way, there was nothing jovial about her. To the contrary, she was filled with fear and her whole body cringed as if she'd been struck. But she'd snap out of it in a moment. Arthur wouldn't. When his mother got that detached, stricken look about her, he grew very silent and some-times wouldn't talk for days, except to David.

My brother, because of the darkness of his skin, had a difficult time making friends. I was only two years older, but even when I was eight, I filled the house with children. David never had a single friend in his early years. Until Arthur. In Arthur, David found acceptance for the first time and Arthur, who only spoke in whispered monosyllables when he came to us, began to talk and grow chatty. He and David were soon inseparable. I had to walk them to kindergarten every morning and home at noon and it mortified me to be with them. Older boys shouted 'nigger' and in winter clobbered them with snowballs. I always stayed a few feet away from them and they huddled together. Occasionally a fourth or fifth grader dragged one of them into a snow drift and the other would beat against the older boy's back.

In the afternoons the boys stayed in the playroom above the garage. It was strange because they never fought. They shared toys, crayons, and the blackboard. They leaned over one another's shoulder to look at a picture book together. I think their calm must have somehow enraged me. I took great pleasure in finding ways to disrupt them. For instance once I got them to take off all their clothes and run through the neighbor's yard while they were having a barbecue. The two dark boys ran naked, screaming while the neighbor's teenaged sons chased them home. Afterwards, my mother punished me for being cruel; I had offered the boys all kinds of rewards if they performed this stunt. 'You don't treat your own kind that way,' my mother said to me. 'Charity begins at home. You must be nice to them.'

'He's not my brother,' I called back to her, 'he's adopted. People often asked if my brother was adopted. Once my father and mother drove three hundred miles to David's summer camp to prove to a cabin full of Jewish ten-year-olds that David did not belong to any racial minority, other than the one we already belonged to. When I shouted that my brother was adopted, my mother climbed up into a closet and dug for our birth certificates. When she found them, she sat me down and together we went over every word. The ones I couldn't read she helped me with until for the first time it actually seemed possible that he was my brother and her child.

But it didn't help very much, her showing me the official reports. There are some things that enter a child's mind that will never leave you as an adult. I walked into the upstairs playroom one day, a dark, grey afternoon, and my brother and Arthur were playing Batman. Both had long blue capes and black masks and they flew around the room in wild, swooshing movements. I stood still in the doorway, searching for some feature that would enable me to tell them apart, but at that moment their skin, their hair, their lips, all that was not concealed, were the same.

After Lillian was with us for several months, it was summer and time for a party for the Jewish Federation. Every summer my mother gave a party to raise funds for displaced persons. Lillian seemed to love the house before the party and she smiled into the silver as she polished it. My mother gave Arthur a seersucker suit of my brother's to wear. Lillian was in charge of hot fudge. It was a beautiful night for a party and the Japanese lanterns glowed and mosquito bombs on the tables kept the bugs away.

Years later my mother told me that that night a woman whom she'd never seen before and wouldn't see again came up to her just as dessert was being served. My mother usually didn't know any of the guests; the Federation simply sent her the list of people they'd invited. 'I just want to let you know, Mrs. Moses, that I think this is very wonderful of you.'

'Oh,' my mother smiled, 'I don't mind doing this to help the Federation.'

'Oh, no,' the woman said, 'I don't mean that. I just think it's so wonderful of you,' pointing to my brother who stood near Lillian as she served, 'to invite your help's children.'

'That,' my mother said flatly, 'is my child.'

Though my mother was certain Lillian had not heard them, it was shortly afterward that Lillian began to change. For me, from summer to winter remains a blur, but I remember clearly the day my mother went to visit my living grandmother in the city. She left Lillian money to take us to eat at Sonny Boy's Delicatessen. It was winter and it got dark very early so Lillian and the boys met me at four o'clock when I left school. The wind was sharp and it was already almost night as we trudged through the snow toward the center of town. Lillian clutched the boys to her while I walked behind. She kept calling to me, 'Now catch up, you hear, child' and 'Now come and walk with us, don't stay so far away I can't see you,' but I kept finding excuses to look into shop windows or call after a stray cat so that I could stay behind them. When we got to the deli, Lillian walked straight back to the restaurant part with Arthur and David. There was a line of people waiting so I stayed near the cash register in the front of the store, watching the snow that was beginning to fall.

Mrs. Sonny, as we called her since we never knew their real last name, spoke with a thick Jewish accent and had long hairs growing from her chin. Both Mr. and Mrs. Sonny had blue numbers tattooed on their arms and so did their daughter, Rachel, who was only seventeen. My father always bought his Sunday morning lox and whitefish from Sonny's because he said it was a miracle they'd survived in Germany and he didn't want them to perish from bankruptcy in Illinois. The lighting was not very good in the restaurant in back and Rachel kept seating people who came in after us. I could hear Rachel's piercing voice as she called the names of waiting parties. She never seemed to have a table for four. Lillian motioned for me to come up and stand with them. I shook my head, pretending to be very interested in the racks of salami, the refrigerator of dead fish.

Finally Lillian must have grown impatient because I saw her touch Rachel on the arm. The girl jerked her arm away. 'Excuse me,' I heard her speak rather loudly, 'but I believe we were here before those people.' Lillian pointed politely to a group that had just been seated.

'Look,' Rachel said, 'we're pretty busy tonight. Maybe if you'd come back tomorrow.'

I found myself crouching in the corner, not wanting anyone to know I was with them, but that only made Mrs. Sonny notice me. She peered down at me from behind the cash register. Then she looked in the direction of Lillian and the two boys. Suddenly she caught me by the arm and was dragging me down to where they were. 'What are you doing?' Mrs. Sonny called to Rachel. 'These are Mrs. Moses' children.'

First Rachel looked confused, then shocked, and finally ter-

ribly apologetic. 'I didn't realize you were Mrs. Moses' girl,'
Rachel said, which for Lillian was the final indignity.

'I ain't nobody's girl, young lady,' Lillian spoke very firmly.
She wasn't shouting and she pulled herself up very tall. She
took David in one hand and Arthur and myself in her other and
while Mrs. Sonny and Rachel called after us, drawing the attention of the whole deli on themselves, Lillian took us from the
store. But Mrs. Sonny ran after us, yelling first apologies and
pleas that we come back and then curses. Her voice shattered
the winter quiet. 'That's the last time I'll do anything to help
out any of you people.'

We walked the mile home in the snow and I don't think I'd
ever been so close to Arthur. Our hands were bound together in
Lillian's fist and even through our mittens, I felt him struggling
to get away from me. But as he struggled, Lillian just clutched
us tighter, almost dragging us. When Arthur realized that he
would have to touch me for the entire walk home, he turned
and stared into my eyes. It was as if he were recording me
forever in his memory, as if there were something about me he
never wanted to forget. I tried to imitate his stare but I lacked
the feeling he obviously had, which I've come to recognize as
hatred. After staring at me for I don't know how long, he finally
spoke more words to me than he'd ever spoken. 'What's the
matter,' he said, 'you don't like being with us?'

Lillian made us cold turkey sandwiches which we ate in silence. Then, when the dishes were washed and there wasn't
anything left for her to clean or arrange, she went into the den
and closed the sliding doors. David and Arthur went to the
upstairs playroom, which was next to my room, and they
weren't in there long when a fight started. They yelled at each
other because one of them had written over what the other had
written on the blackboard. It was the first time they ever fought
and, for some reason, I couldn't bear to hear it and I covered
my ears with my palms. Downstairs Lillian remained absolutely
quiet in the den but at eight-thirty on the dot, when it was time
to put us to bed, the sliding doors were opened. From my room,
I could always see the shadow as someone moved up the stairs

and I saw that Lillian was having trouble walking. In fact she was almost crawling, using her hands to support herself as she moved up the stairs, and she was talking to Abel with each step. 'You did this to us, Abel. You brought that boy into the world and you made him see this.'

When she reached the top of the stairs, I slammed my books shut and dove into bed but she passed my room. She lumbered into the playroom like a huge beast and, mumbling under her breath, she put everything away. David and Arthur dashed past her as if somehow they knew to get out of her way. They rushed to get ready for bed and, when we were all settled in, Lillian turned off every light in the house and every outdoor light and the downstairs hallway light. She made the house pitch black and through the blackness I heard her call, 'And now you children, now you can all go to sleep.'

A glare of light woke me abruptly. 'Are you all right? Where's your brother? Is he all right?' My parents were rushing through the house, illuminating it like a Christmas tree. David cried as they woke him, checking him from head to toe to make sure he was all right. Lillian opened the door to her room; 'What's all the fuss about?' she called, her voice sluggish from sleep.

'Why aren't there any lights on?' my father shouted. They had never come home to a dark house before.

The next day after lunch my mother drove David to a neighbor's house to play with their children. And every afternoon from then on, my mother arranged for him to go to the house of some child who was in his class at school. Often David protested that he wanted to stay home and be with Arthur but my mother always said, 'You can spend the evening with Arthur.' It was not long before David had made many new friends and Arthur again stayed close to his mother, following her in his silence through the house.

My grandmother was rushed to the hospital on a Saturday afternoon and my parents suddenly had to go to the city. They told Lillian to keep us at home and that they'd be back before nightfall. Lillian went into my father's den after they left and closed the sliding doors. When she emerged almost an hour later, she was more jovial than I'd seen her in months and she said we were going to the zoo. She got us dressed. Though it was the beginning of spring, there was still a nip in the air so she bundled us up and we walked hand-in-hand up Hazel Avenue to the train station. We walked four abreast in the middle of the road and when cars whizzed past us, honking very loud, Lillian laughed and said, 'I feel like a crusader, leading you children along.' She laughed louder than usual and her feet kept staggering so from side to side that at times I was sure she would fall. All I could think of was how would we pick her up if she fell and how would we keep a car from running over her if we couldn't pick her up.

When we got to the zoo, everyone wanted to see everything but in a different order so Lillian agreed that we would systematically visit, talk to, and feed every animal in the Lincoln Park Zoo. At the Children's Zoo we gaped at baby polar bears for almost half an hour and Arthur and David let a boa constrictor wrap itself around their shoulders. The giraffe reached down from her cage and took peanuts from my hand and in the monkey house we all stood in front of the mirror, jumping up and down, under the sign which read 'World's Most Dangerous Animal.' Whatever we wanted to eat, Lillian bought for us. To this day I don't know where the money came from. When it started to get dark, we took a cab to the train and the 5:15 home. It was the fast train that my father always took from work and we felt very official. We acted important and whispered jokes to one another. When we walked into the house, my mother was sitting in a chair in the den, crying, and my father had the phone in his hand. He told Lillian that he was just going to phone the police.

A few days later, on Lillian's day off, I found my father in the den. He had taken all the liquor out of the bar and all the bottles were lined up on the floor. 'Are we having a party?' I asked because before a party, he always took all the liquor out and, like a chemist, funneled the almost-empty bottles in the almost-full bottles. My father was a great consolidator and he loved to make things simple and compact.

'No, we aren't having a party,' he mumbled back to me.

Later that day my parents closed the doors to the den and all I could hear was my father, his voice rising, saying, 'That's the last thing we need in this house. I'd rather have a slut than a drunk. At least a slut doesn't do it on the premises.' And with that, my mother told him to calm down and I couldn't hear any more.

That night as I lay asleep, my door opened and Lillian, her bulk filling the doorway, stood still for a moment. Then she began rocking back and forth, right there in the doorway. Then she came to me. She gripped me to her breasts and sang 'Hush Little Baby'; she covered me with her body so that I could hardly breathe and I felt her hot breath against my neck.

The next morning, when we went downstairs for breakfast, they were gone. My mother sat us down and explained that it was all for the best and they didn't have time to say good-bye. They had taken the early morning train back to Meridian because Lillian, my mother said, missed her people.

Almost twenty years later I was walking through Chicago's Loop at Christmastime. Above me the elevated trains clanged; the snow which had fallen the night before was black with soot. My arms ached from the packages I carried and I don't remember a day being so cold. I dashed into Schrafft's for a cup of coffee and a club sandwich. While waiting in a booth for my sandwich to come, I noticed a man staring at me from the soda counter. I looked back at him for a moment and saw he had a beautiful, almost sculpted face and dark, sullen eyes. He was black. I looked away from him but he didn't look away from me and after a while I felt very uncomfortable and annoyed. I began to stare back at him, thinking it would force him to turn away, but instead it locked us in an awkward gaze. Trying to break away from him, I made my eyes move down to his feet and studied his hiking boots, his tight, bleached jeans, his bulky fisherman's sweater, the blue parka which fell over his shoulders. When my eyes returned to his face, I saw that he had not stopped looking at me. Suddenly he rose from his stool, gathered up the packages which lay at his feet and walked over to my table. Then he spoke, very formally. 'Excuse me for staring at you, but are you Miss Moses? Deborah Moses?' I nodded and he held out his hand. 'Arthur Jackson,' he said.

I motioned for him to sit down, which he did. He ordered a cup of coffee and asked the waitress to add it to his bill from the counter. 'What are you doing back North?' I asked, suddenly regretting that those were the first words out of my mouth.

He had a pleasant smile and wasn't at all like the retiring boy I had known. He looked at me strangely but laughing, 'I'm afraid we never did get out of the North. Why?' I shook my head, not knowing what to say next, afraid that what I would say would somehow be wrong. But he did the talking. Lillian had died, he told me, ten years ago. A black family had let him live with them. He pointed to the gifts which lay at his feet. 'They're for them,' he said. He referred to the family as 'his people.' Arthur was graduating from the University of Illinois in the spring and was going to medical school downstate.

'That's wonderful,' I said. My sandwich had arrived but I hadn't noticed it.

'And you?' he asked. He was leaning forward and I felt him giving me his full attention. I'd been out of school for two years and was planning to go to law school the next fall but I found I didn't want to discuss myself or my future. I wanted to know about Arthur, but I didn't want him to know anything about me. Hoping to change the subject, I said, 'How did you ever recognize me?'

He laughed, 'You've hardly changed at all. And those eyes. I'd never forget them.' Looking back, I'm sure he meant that as a compliment but at the moment I thought he was referring to the night when we went to Sonny Boy's, and I couldn't bring myself to look at him again until he said, 'I'd like to see David. Is he around?'

I shrugged, feeling somewhat annoyed that he'd brought up David at that moment. 'He should be coming home for Christmas, but with David you never know. He's a musician out East. A saxophonist.'

Arthur whistled through his teeth, obviously impressed. I

wrote down our home phone number for him. 'Call David,' I said. 'Next week. Probably he'll get here and I'm sure he'd love to hear from you.' Arthur took the slip of paper from me with David's number and started buttoning his parka. 'I live on the North Side,' I added, 'Near Evanston with some friends. Why don't you drop in sometime?' He nodded and said he would but he did not ask for my number nor did he offer me his. 'Why don't you give me your number,' I said, adding quickly, 'so I can have David call you when he gets here?'

'I would but my people don't have a phone.' I nodded but found myself feeling profoundly disappointed that Arthur had not asked how to get in touch with me. I felt helpless because I could not reach him if I wanted to. Someone opened the door to Schrafft's wide and a cold wind blew in, mixed with snow. We each wrapped our arms around ourselves and shivered. I wanted to urge him to call me. I almost wanted to beg him to see me, but he was already standing up and all I managed to say was, 'So you didn't move back to Mississippi?'

He shook his head. He seemed in a hurry to go somewhere. 'To be honest, I don't remember a thing about Mississippi.' Arthur scooped up his bundles and my check. 'It's funny. I remember your eyes but I don't remember where I spent the first six years of my life. This is my home.' I was reaching for my check, which seemed to flutter in his hand like a bird, but he shook his head. 'Let me get this,' and he was already at the cashier's paying my bill. I waved at him and he blew me a kiss. The snow was coming down as Arthur opened the door, heading back to the South Side where it seemed he'd been living for all those years.

When he opened the door, another cold breeze blew in and again I shivered. I rubbed my hands briskly up and down my arms. Then I remembered why I'd gone into Lillian's room so long ago. My mother had left the window open and I woke up feeling cold, so cold my head ached. As I caught a last glimpse of Arthur, walking against the wind, I remembered him lying there in that dark, warm room and how it felt to lie with them, arms and legs all wrapped together like a package.

The Glass Wall

❦

ROSA RESTED ON THE STEPS of the Cookie Dream Factory, her mother's bakery, wondering why Uncle Tio's pet pig ran away two nights ago. The moon had been full when Uncle Tio opened the door of their house, peering in with red eyes to inquire if they'd seen the old pink-and-black sow he'd never had the guts to slaughter, whom he called Petunia. She was a destructive pig, eating clothes and ripping out fences. Every year she ruined the vegetable patch, but what else did Uncle Tio have but that rambled-down shack, his sledgehammer, and the dried-up sow? Rosa shuffled the lottery tickets she held in her hand, staring at the numbers; no one had bought from her all day. She told Uncle Tio that if she won the lottery, she'd buy him a new pig but he just shook his head, disappearing back into the shadows of the alleyway as he fumbled along toward his shack. He wanted the old pig.

Trapper's jeep pulled up and Rosa saw he had two men with him, tourists from across the border, probably from the East, who came to hunt. Trapper led them into the high country. Rosa's mother, Dolores Two-Step, slumped on a ratty armchair in the back of the bakery, watching a soap opera she'd been following for seven years, thinking some day it would end. When the jeep drove up, Dolores moved to the front of the store while Rosa shouted back that it was just Trapper with some more men. Trapper squeezed her shoulder the way he did once or

twice a week when he made these rounds. He'd bring the tourists into town for supplies and always he'd see Rosa, not like he used to, but he'd always pass by the store.

The three men walked into Dolores Two-Step's Cookie Dream Factory. They called her Two-Step because her word was like poison from a two-step snake, but in the Cookie Dream Factory, she hardly spoke. Trapper kissed her on the cheek calling her Tia, even though he knew she was angry with him. He always brought his hunters here to buy bread because he knew they needed the money and because it was a big tourist attraction – the only real tourist attraction in town, outside of a visit to the nuclear reactor and the abandoned silver mine, each an hour away in opposite directions. Dolores extracted sugar from fruits and made cookies out of ground flour and these she shaped into objects. People came in, thinking they'd get chocolate chip or peanut butter cookies but they grew entranced with the funny objects, sculpted from dough, which were supposed to predict the future. Dolores watched as the eyes of the men scanned the strange pouncing animals, the wild sprawling trees, the shanties, the little villages and their cookie denizens. To the tall man, she gave a fireman cookie, saying he was a man of great passion and would always be loved. To the stocky man, she gave a deer cookie and said he was going on a long journey that would prove profitable. And to Trapper she gave a tree cookie, as she had consistently for the past three months, saying he'd be buried under one soon.

The stocky man slapped his friend on the back; he'd just gotten a transfer last week to his bank's Tokyo branch. The tall man smirked a little, casually admitting that he was very passionate, letting his gaze fall on Rosa as she sat on the front steps. Then they both glanced morbidly at Trapper, asking if her predictions ever came true. 'All the time.' He munched on his tree cookie and Dolores gave him another, glancing over her shoulder to see what was happening with her soap opera. It was six months and still no one knew where the doctor's daughter had gone or with whom.

Trapper was eating a prairie dog and a policeman when Rosa wandered in. 'Uncle Tio's on the hill.'

Trapper went to the entranceway, looking up in the direction of Uncle Tio. 'What's he doing?' he mumbled.

'Petunia ran away two nights ago,' Rosa replied. In the distance Uncle Tio groped his way further and further up the hill.

The tourists wanted more dream cookies but Trapper told them they only got one shot. Trapper kissed Dolores on the cold cheek which she turned quickly away from him. He walked to the porch with Rosa behind him and put his arm on her shoulder but she moved away. Lately everyone he touched moved away. He was starting to get used to it. But Rosa knew Trapper, knew him like the back of her hand, with the instinct that animals know and fear one another. He was Trapper because that's what he did, caught poor helpless things. He was also El Negro because he was black inside and out, and no one knew it like Rosa because she'd known him since they were three. She knew him in the woods, in the dark; many nights his skins had kept her warm and she still slept draped in the fox, the beaver, the raccoon, left over from a time when she'd done anything to stay warm. He yearned for her and she knew that. She knew that depriving him was the worst thing she could do and deprive him she did. And she knew that as long as she deprived him, he'd keep passing by the store. It was the only way to keep him.

The stocky man took a Coke from the Coke machine and the tall man took an orange drink. Sweat poured down their necks, moistening their collars. The tall man wiped his neck with a handkerchief as he drank the orange drink.

'Tell Uncle Tio I'll look for Petunia on the road up to the mountains,' Trapper said, swinging back into the jeep. He was huge and brawny, with enormous feet. Rosa smiled, trying to imagine the pig taking a road somewhere.

'Maybe we should let her come along to cook for us,' the tall man joked, gloating over the fact that Dolores Two-Step had called him a passionate man.

'Shut up,' Trapper mumbled under his breath but loud enough so Rosa could hear, 'I loved that girl once.'

Dolores Two-Step always left the bakery early because that's what she'd done when her husband was alive and because she was accustomed to getting dinner. It was eight-thirty when Rosa closed the Cookie Dream Factory. She closed at the same time every night. Then she took a few pesos from the till and bought two lottery tickets, one for herself and one for El Negrito. Sometimes, if they had a good day, she bought more. Sometimes she even bought one which she mentally gave to Trapper but she never told anyone.

It was dark in the night and the skies were very black because the full moon had passed when Rosa set out on her way home. In Esperanza they say that if you fall to the ground, you go to hell, and that if a dog barks all night at the moon, he talks to the devil. Even though Rosa wasn't superstitious, ever since Petunia ran away, some yellow dog had been barking all night, and the night before on her way home, Rosa had tripped over something in the road and fallen. She didn't quite hit the ground but her hands did and she wondered if only her hands could go to hell. And just last night, she'd seen a cat with the face of a child sitting on a wall.

There were two ways to go home. Her barrio was San Rafael and she could take the long way, up toward the highway near where her brother had been killed, then cut over to the Calle Zapata, down the cobble streets, and up the very steep hill to the Calle Hidalgo which had the wall around it. This way was almost three miles and she didn't get home until well after nine. Then there was the other way, the way she came every day when she went to work for the Señora and the way she walked home when she came back late every night. It was the easy way, it was the way she liked, not because it was easy and the path was smooth but because it took her past people's houses and not only along the dark streets and she felt safer. This way, which she walked along now, took her home as the crow flies. She would cut through the Colonia Riodoro, following a straight path until she came to the wall. In the wall there was a hole, and when they built Riodoro two years ago, they had left the hole in the wall, and this was the way people who lived in San Rafael went home.

As she walked along the dirt path through Riodoro, she looked at the houses. She liked to look at these white and pink houses which at night looked even bigger than they did in the day. In San Rafael, the houses were all very small, just piles of wooden slats and sometimes cement, and chickens and donkeys walked all around the houses, but here there weren't any animals making noise and walking around and the paths were very clean. In San Rafael, you could see the lights from fires but the houses were dark and cold and when she looked at the houses in San Rafael, she didn't feel warm the way she did when she walked through Riodoro. But she never could see the whole house. Each house was hidden behind a stucco wall or row of hedges followed by a stucco wall, and if she didn't work for the Señora, she wouldn't know what it was like inside. Rosa always liked to see the lights on in other people's houses. She pictured big dogs, a man by the fire, a couple snuggled in bed. She liked to walk in the dark night and look into the windows, to see silhouettes moving inside, and sometimes as she walked by, she would see them looking down at her from behind their picture windows and she knew that in the daytime from those windows they could see across the whole valley, to the border even. She had to climb the steep hill in order to see that far. And now as she walked, she saw people looking down at her from the picture windows, noses pressed to the glass.

A dog kept howling somewhere and that made her nervous. She looked down at the ground, careful not to fall. It was late and she was going to be late getting home, which meant she might not see El Negrito until the following evening, because when she left in the morning he was usually still asleep. She'd reached the wall. The short way took her fifteen minutes to walk from the bakery to the wall and another fifteen from the wall to her house. If she were lucky and hurried, she could put him to bed herself.

She reached the wall and stared. For a long time she stared and stared. She touched it. The stone in front of her was a paler shade and the cement between the stones wasn't quite dry. It took several minutes for her to understand that there was no more hole, no way to pass through. Someone had closed the hole so that the people who lived in San Rafael could no longer take the shortcut through Riodoro. Rosa looked at the houses behind her, the lights coming from the windows, the few faces staring down. She wondered if they could see her from where they stood. She assumed some could see her but most couldn't. The wall wasn't that high, only five feet or so, and there were stones lying on the ground in front of where the hole had been. If she turned and went back she'd be another hour getting home. She climbed up on a rock, hoisted herself onto the wall and flew over, landing hard on the cobblestone like a heavy bird, careful not to let anything but her feet touch the ground. Rosa gasped, catching her breath as she landed. It was day on one side and night on the other. The San Rafael barrio was almost pitch black with no street lights on the cobble walk, except for the light that came from a few houses set back off the road. The Colonia Riodoro was always lighter than the barrio San Rafael but she'd never quite noticed it as she did at that moment.

She walked up the Calle Hidalgo. Whenever it looks as if things could be getting easier, something makes them harder, she thought. It was just two months ago when she got the job with the Señora and could stop selling Kleenex out by the intersection where her brother had gotten run over by the dump truck. And that was after that very bad time when her mother told her about Trapper and the woman up north and when El Negrito was born. She climbed the hill slowly, feet clicking against the cobblestone. I'm not afraid, she told herself. This is the only part of my walk home when I could be afraid because it's so dark here and there are walls on both sides and no place to go if someone jumps out at me like that crazy Naranjo boy did that night, but I was with Trapper who was taking a leak in the bushes a few yards back. Never saw anyone jump so high as the Naranjo boy when Trapper came up behind him and thrust his pocket knife up against his spine. This is the only part of the walk that's bad, the last stretch or so up the hill on the road that's walled in on both sides. Otherwise there's no problem at all. Rosa walked straight on, not looking over her shoulder, not wanting to see if anyone was behind her or to the side of her or standing on the wall peering down at her.

Uncle Tio brought his sledgehammer down hard on a new pole for his fence as Rosa walked by. Everyone knew that 'uncle' meant 'tio' and 'tio' meant 'uncle' and that his name didn't mean anything, but Uncle Tio was all mixed up because their house had straddled the border in Nogales when he was born. He was no one's uncle that anyone knew about but he belonged to everyone in San Rafael and that's what they'd called him since before Rosa was born. He paused, stared blankly at Rosa, then raised the sledgehammer and brought it down again. It was how Uncle Tio spent most of his nights, hammering new fences to keep his chickens in. All the chickens had names that Rosa could never keep straight. If you went to Uncle Tio's for dinner, he'd often say, 'We're eating Cyclone tonight.' Or Redhead or Henpecked. There was something strange about eating an animal whose name you knew but Uncle Tio talked about Cyclone or Redhead as he ate them, discussing the kind of life they'd lived right up until the end. He brought the sledgehammer down again, then turned to Rosa.

'Uncle Tio, they filled up the hole in the wall. Why do you suppose they did that?'

Uncle Tio shrugged his shoulders. 'Have you seen my pig?' he asked.

The next morning before dawn Rosa walked around the wall to go to the Colonia Riodoro because she was afraid she'd get caught. When she got to work the Señora told her she had to go to the dentist in El Paso for the day and might not be back the next day either. The Señora had married a Mexican who gave her two children before he married her, and half the town, too, the half that had running water, by the time he died. The Señora paid her almost three dollars for the morning's work, and the only thing Rosa didn't like was that she wouldn't let Rosa in the house unless she was there to watch her, so when the Señora went to El Paso Rosa didn't get paid. The next morning Rosa jumped the wall but the Señora was still in El Paso and the next day too so Rosa only worked at the bakery those days and sold lottery tickets when she was done baking. And at the end of the day she sat alone in the bakery, listening to the night sounds - boys dribbling basketballs up and down the street, Uncle Tio hollering about his lost pig, cars whizzing by on their way to Texas.

The third morning, the morning when the Señora came home and Rosa went back to work, she saw men working on the wall so she had to walk around. It was only six in the morning when she passed where the hole had been and she saw them, preparing to do some work. It didn't look like they were going to make the hole back again because they had plaster with them. That morning Dolores took El Negrito to the bakery because Juana, Rosa's older sister who had twins and had been nursing El Negrito while Rosa worked, had something wrong with her throat and didn't know if she could nurse her own until she got back from the clinic. Rosa carried the baby in her arms and her mother hobbled along beside her. Dolores Two-Step, as sharp as was her tongue, had bad ankles and often fell on the cobblestones so Rosa never let her carry El Negrito when they took him somewhere. Everyone knew that Dolores wouldn't go to hell for falling because she had special connections and powers no one else could understand but which they all believed in. Dolores looked at the place where the hole had once been in the wall and spat on the ground in front of the men who were arranging their plaster and tools on the ground. The workers were sons of friends, all from the barrio San Rafael, and she looked at them as she spat and they didn't say anything to her because they knew Dolores could put a curse on anyone she wanted.

When Rosa reached the house, the Señora was waiting for her. She complained that Rosa was late and she had been waiting for almost half an hour. 'I didn't know if you'd be here,' Rosa said. 'I came the other days and you weren't here so I didn't know.'

The Señora was angry. 'If you don't want to work, there are other girls who do,' the Señora said, but Rosa didn't say anything back because she needed the three dollars a day.

'It's because of the wall,' Rosa said. 'They filled in the hole in the wall and I have to walk around.'

'What are you talking about?' the Señora asked. 'What hole?'

Rosa was sitting in the back of the bakery, cutting animal cookies for the Dream Factory with El Negrito sleeping on the couch, when she heard the jeep drive up. She heard the sound of footsteps coming up the steps of the bakery. She knew as the jeep pulled around the corner, she knew from the way it shrieked on its tires, from the way it pulled to a halt, from the way the door slammed and the feet climbed the steps, that it was Trapper and he was drunk. She heard him pacing the front of the bakery but she kept cutting her animal cookies. Then she heard him tapping his fingers, calling, moving behind the counter. He opened the curtain and stepped into the back room. She was watching Kung Fu and did not take her eyes from the set.

Trapper walked in and slumped onto the couch beside El Negrito. He patted the baby on the head like a dog, he caressed its cheek. Rosa watched carefully, not saying a word. She watched to make sure he didn't touch the boy too hard. Slowly Trapper looked her way. He was a somber man with curly black hair and very black eyes. His body was firm and Rosa's, he always told her, was soft and plump. Trapper spent the years of his youth trying to prove his prowess by arm wrestling as often as possible in Rosa's presence. His skin always looked dirty even if he'd just bathed and no matter how long he slept he always seemed tired. When he was a boy, she remembered, he had few friends and mostly kept to himself, unless he was playing games with her. When they played doctor, he always had some invisible ailment she could never cure.

He looked up at her and sighed. 'I'll marry you,' he muttered. 'That's what I came to say.'

She shook her head. He looked at her hard and she knew what he was thinking. She can be stubborn if she wants. Sometimes he hated her. Sometimes he went up into the hills when the fish were biting or it was time for the rut and never wanted to see her again. He rose and took from the oven some donuts that had just finished baking. He took milk from the refrigerator. He knew where everything was. He sat across from her. 'We can get married. All right? Is that what you want?'

'Leave me alone,' she said softly but emphatically.

He ate a donut whole, popping it into his mouth. 'You don't understand, do you? I can't live without you. I don't want to live without you. There's no woman up north and if there was, there isn't now and won't be again. I want to be with you. I want to live with you. I can't stand it any more.'

She was beginning to enjoy depriving him and that worried her. It had become a sacred mission in her life, to deny him. It had become some wonderful, fantastically contrived test of will and now it was no longer a test but the most natural thing in the world. As long as she could earn ten dollars a day, she didn't need him. She loved him and always would but she'd never need him again, not the way she had. Juana said she was a fool. 'Marry him,' she yelled at her in the evenings. 'What else are you going to do with your life?'

'I want you to go away,' she spoke firmly. 'I don't want you any more.'

He fumbled with a piece of dough on the long wooden table, twisting it into a million shapes, grabbing cookie cutters and cutting it into houses and dogs and flowers and rivers and trees and cars, into all the things he liked and couldn't stand, the things he wanted or could have been. He made a Coke bottle and smashed it. He made tourists and the Grand Canyon. He made a woman and smashed her. He made a baby and smashed it. Rosa sat and watched him move as if his life were going by in a swift succession. Then he took the dough, rolled it up in his hand and hurled it onto the table as if it were dice, and smashed it into a pancake so flat and thin that Rosa could almost read the newspaper headlines that lay underneath. Then he leaned forward, perched on his knuckles like a great ape, and stared her square in the eye. 'What do I have to do?' Rosa didn't know what he had to do. She didn't know if she wanted him to do anything. 'What do I have to do?' He slammed his fist onto the pancake dough, then held his palm out to her like a beggar pleading for alms, his face twisted like the dough in rage and humiliation.

Rosa paused and thought for a moment. 'Blow up the wall,' she mumbled.

'What wall?' Trapper looked around him, thinking it might be nearby. 'What are you talking about!'

'The wall that's in my way,' she said. 'The one that blocks the shortcut; the one that makes me late for work.'

He reached across and tried to grab her. He put his hand against her shirt and tried to pull her to him. She pushed him away. 'And don't touch me,' she shouted, pointing at him. 'Don't touch me until you blow up that wall.'

'Is that all?'

She nodded. 'And drive me home.'

Trapper took the road through town, swung around and circled past Riodoro, then drove up Insurgentes until he came to Calle Hidalgo. It was much faster in a car, Rosa thought. Maybe she should marry him so he could bring her home in the car. A month ago she would have married him; a week ago maybe; but suddenly now she wouldn't marry him for all the money in the world, unless he put a hole back in the wall for her. A hole she'd never use because she'd marry him and he'd drive her home every night in the jeep and drive her to work every morning in it too. She looked at Trapper from the side without really looking at him. There were two kinds of people to her. The kind who were dark and you couldn't see into them at all; then there was the other kind, the ones who were transparent and you could see everything. Even when they tried they couldn't hide what they felt. Trapper was the see-through kind. Her mother was the opaque kind. There was a part of her that was proud she now could get Trapper to do exactly what she wanted, after so many years of waiting for him to come around. Now that she didn't care.

They were driving past the wall and suddenly she saw the bright, shimmering fragments in the moonlight - lime green, a soft, coffee brown, a bright yellow gold, and white, and an almost blood red. They were shiny and pointed and they stuck up in the moonlight like cactus on the prairie. She grabbed Trapper's hand on the shift and motioned for him to stop. 'That wall?' he said, watching as Rosa stared, then jumped down from the jeep. 'Is that the wall?' She walked over to the wall, El Negrito in her arms. She let her hands slide over the sharp, pointed shards of glass which stuck out of the still-moist plaster on the top of the wall and along the sloping sides, glass from Coke bottles and Seven-Up bottles, bright blue mineral water and dull brown beer bottles, broken on barroom floors, Fanta and Pepsi Cola, glass from the bottles she drank all day, bottles from companies her people didn't own. In the moonlight the wall shimmered and the light that passed over the fragments turned into stars. It shone like those wonderful rocks Trapper used to bring down from the mountains and chop in half so that inside you saw crystals of all colors and shapes that had been hidden inside there for so many centuries, growing inside the rock. And it stood up like shark's fins, bright and wet out of the water. The men had put pieces of sharp glass along the top of the wall so that the people who lived in San Rafael couldn't jump the wall on their way to and from town where most of them worked and so that the streets of Riodoro would be very clean. Rosa let her fingers run over the glass, feeling the sharp edges biting at her hand. Then she climbed back into the jeep. Trapper drove along. 'So, as soon as the hunters leave, I'll get some dynamite and knock a hole big enough for an elephant to pass through.'

The next morning Rosa walked around the wall and lost her job. She'd gotten up at five-thirty but El Negrito was sick and she didn't want to leave him until Uncle Tio, who once worked on an ambulance, came to take a look. She left her house at seven but didn't reach the Señora until after eight. 'You're erratic,' the Señora said. 'I don't like undependable people.' She said there were other things too that she didn't like about the way Rosa did things and she closed the door. For a few moments

Rosa stood staring at the door, then she spat at it the way her mother had taught her to do, putting a curse she knew wouldn't work because she didn't have the power her mother had.

Late that night when she was making dough, Trapper walked into the store. He startled her because she hadn't heard his jeep drive up and she hadn't heard his footsteps as he walked into the store; he'd come in silently like an Indian. She jumped up. She pushed her hand over her chest and felt her heart pounding inside. Usually when he came in he made a big noise. Usually she could hear him a mile away.

He didn't say anything but moved silently through the back of the bakery, moving around and around in circles. He pounded his fist into cupboards, on counters and tabletops; Rosa moved back. 'You're drunk.' She saw, as he moved toward her, that he was worse than he'd been the night before.

'I'm going to take El Negrito away,' he said, still moving toward her while she kept backing up against the wall. On the counter there was a knife and slowly she worked her way toward it. The baby started crying, his face turning blue. Trapper slammed his fist into the wall, into the cupboard. He moved beside where she stood at the counter and Rosa reached behind her back for the knife. She pulled the knife in front of her and stared at him. Then suddenly Trapper leaned his head against the counter and started to cry. He sobbed big heavy sobs so that his whole body shook and when Rosa thought he was done, he started again with heavier sobs. She picked up El Negrito and went to Trapper who now cried silently, his mouth open in a grotesque laugh which brought tears down his cheeks and from which no sound came. Rosa went to him, wrapping his head up with her hands and pulling him close to her. 'I wouldn't take him away,' he mumbled through his sobs. 'But you're making me crazy.' She wanted to say that he never wanted her when she wanted him, she wanted to say that he never was there when she needed him, but there was something about seeing him, sobbing against her chest, that made her stop thinking those things. Suddenly she wanted him again, not as she'd wanted him before, not the kind of wanting that made it so she

couldn't sleep but the kind that made her want to sit by a big
fire with him at her side. 'As soon as the hunters leave,' he said,
'I'll blow up the wall.' Trapper was very good with dynamite.

Just before dawn the tall passionate man was startled from
his restless sleep and, without thinking, shot Trapper through
the shoulder as he made his way back to their campsite. The
stocky man, who didn't want any trouble with the authorities,
stuffed some money into Trapper's shirt pocket, took his jeep,
and headed for the border. It took Trapper a full day to make
it down the mountain on foot to Dolores Two-Step's cabin.
When he staggered in, Dolores screamed as she had when her
oldest boy was killed, and nothing could convince her that
Trapper wasn't going to die.

When Rosa walked in after nine, she saw the doctor who
tended the San Rafael people cleaning Trapper's wound and
she saw her mother, tears streaming down her cheeks, heating
herbs on the stove. El Negrito slept peacefully in his crib. Her
first thought was that she hadn't seen the jeep out front and she
knew it was gone. Now she'd have to walk around the wall
forever. Her second thought was disbelief. That one of her
mother's predictions almost came true. And then she thought
that she didn't know what she wanted and she was mad. She
didn't know if she wanted him or not. Last night she wanted
him; suddenly she didn't know. But she didn't want him to die,
she knew that. She walked over to where he lay, breathing
heavily. She touched him and seeing he'd live, she stormed out
of the cabin. She screamed back at him, 'Why didn't you blow
it up when you said you would?' Trapper started to cry again.
She walked down the road until she came to Uncle Tio's shack.
Uncle Tio was out cold, head on the table, drunk, and she took
his sledgehammer from under the table and moved fast down
the road, her feet flying over the cobblestone, dragging the
sledgehammer behind her.

She walked until she came to where the hole had been. She
looked for a moment at where the pale, new cement and stone
met with the old and the new stone took shape next to the old.
First it was a lady, dressed up for church or a parade. Then it

was a jockey, riding his horse fast over the finish. She ran her fingers over the glass as if it were piano keys she was about to play. Then she brought the sledgehammer over her head with both hands and smashed it into the wall. Glass splintered all around her like tiny fish darting through dark water. She closed her eyes tight and brought it down again. She smashed at the sharp edges, grinding them fine as sand. She smashed the way Trapper had smashed dough and she smashed just as easily. The people in Riodoro came to their windows when they heard the sound but no one dared come down and see what was happening. All they saw was the hammerhead coming up and glass flying in tiny, brilliant splinters. She kept at it. When the glass was gone, she worked on the stone. She saw the people staring down at her with darkened faces she could not recognize. She knocked out one stone, then another. She knocked out a hole large enough for a child to pass through. Then she stopped. Trapper could finish the job. She knew she had him where she wanted him now and that he would do this for her. She had broken him as she'd broken the wall.

She started slowly back up the hill, tired this time, dragging the sledgehammer so that it bounced on the cobbles. She stopped when she heard a sound she knew she did not make. At first she thought it was men who'd come to harm her, the ones she'd always feared would hide and jump out at her when she didn't expect it. She thought it was they who'd just pushed their way through the hole she opened in the wall, but she saw nothing. She started walking again, but then she heard the sound again and knew she was being followed. She turned, gripping the hammer, ready to smash whoever it was, when she saw, walking behind her on the last dark stretch of road, Petunia methodically working her way home. From behind their windows of glass, the Riodoro people now watched the pig. Pigs, they say, are smart, and this one, who seemed to recognize either Rosa or the sledgehammer, caught up with her and together they walked the rest of the way up the hill.

The Mark of the Tartars

THE DAY HIS FIRST social security check arrived, my father decided he wouldn't die without seeing the Grand Canyon. He wanted it to be a family outing and en route we were to stop at all the towns along the way where he'd worked in his youth. Gary, Hannibal, Kansas City. A kind of backward journey, retracing the steps that led him to work in the packaging plant outside Milwaukee where we lived. We were to keep a slow but steady westward course until we stood at the rim of the big gaping crevasse and looked in. He papered the living room in triple-A maps. Like all legendary navigators, his eyes grew dark, his skin pale as he stayed up well past the time he usually went to sleep, sticking pins in all the places he wanted to see. Scenic routes, turnpikes, landmarks, river roads.

We didn't want to go. My older brother, Dean, who at seventeen slicked his hair down and smoked cigarettes in front of Leo's delicatessen in the center of town, had made a recent appearance in juvenile court on a drunken driving charge. For years he and my father had been at odds, unable to be in the same room for long. My father could never understand how he got such a son and Dean, whose license was revoked by the judge, would never sit still across the desolate reaches of Midwestern highway. At fifteen, I was in love with a basketball player who walked through the house with a basketball palmed in each hand as if he'd just picked them from a tree; every moment away from him was unbearable to me. Though we hadn't traveled anywhere as a family since I was very small, our mother was in favor. She said it would give us a chance to get to know one another better, but Dean said we knew enough already.

In the end we had no choice. Grandma sat in front, next to my father. She kept drifting to sleep and waking with a jolt. 'Are we there?' She'd gaze dumbly at the tree-lined highway. 'Is this the Petrified Forest?'

'We aren't going to a forest, Ma.' My father patted her hand. 'We're going to the Grand Canyon and won't get there for two weeks.' Then she'd relax, fall back asleep and wake with a jolt, worried that we'd reached the Petrified Forest, muttering about the poor, hardened trees which seemed to frighten her.

Dean sat beside our mother who was crocheting a blanket and he had one leg going up and down at approximately the same speed we were traveling. Mother kept saying, 'Stop it, dear. Relax,' or 'You should get up earlier and exercise,' which only made him accelerate. The blanket was supposed to be a souvenir of our journey, with a little car in the center, scenes of mountains, Old Faithful, and the Alamo, which wasn't even on our itinerary. For reasons of protocol which I didn't entirely understand, I rode in the backward seat of the station wagon which I shared with some luggage and sometimes with Dean whose knees reached to his chin in the backward seat when he changed places to escape our mother. Then he slept with his head bobbing on my shoulder and I kept pushing him up so they wouldn't know he was missing the scenery. When Dean moved in back, I had to stay put while my mother stretched her arms, working on the borders of the blanket, so that my view for the entire trip was of where we'd been, not of where we were going.

But Dean was wrong about what we knew. The details of our father's life weren't known to us at all. What we knew were the generalities. How he'd managed two thousand steel workers in Gary, a department store named J. W. Wenchel's in Hannibal, and had a brief career as a jazz pianist. Once my mother met

a man who said my father played the best Scott Joplin for a 'honky' north of St. Louis and west of Pittsburgh but my father claimed the man confused him with someone else. Still, late at night, when everyone was asleep, I'd hear him at the piano. I'd go downstairs and sit at the bench but he kept playing as if he didn't know I was there.

'What's that?' I asked when he finally paused.

'It used to be "April in Paris" before I fixed it up,' he said, starting in on some new tune. Or it used to be 'Lullaby of Broadway' or 'Yellow Rose of Texas.' The songs he 'fixed up' always seemed to cite geographical locations in their titles, which was strange because he'd never had much interest in travel before. But sometimes he said, 'Oh, that was popular way before you were born.' Sometimes when he played, my mother dragged down the old photo album. I had a difficult time believing they'd lived before I was born and the pictures always were unreal to me. She'd turn the pages, pointing to people in evening clothes on the patio at French Lick whom she said were my parents. To someone she said was my father, with one foot perched on an old Ford, cigarette dangling from his lips, with a wild, laughing woman in the front seat who was not my mother. There was always something a little too jovial about these pictures, which left me feeling uneasy, as if somehow they were hiding something, as if they weren't exactly as they'd presented themselves to be.

Though he rarely spoke about himself, there was one story he told me after someone slighted me so I'd be grateful for what I had. It was about the window dresser at J. W. Wenchel's in Hannibal just after the Depression. He was a crippled black man without any 'people,' as my father referred to family, who walked hunched over, his right hand twisted into a claw. No one was as alone as the window dresser whose name my father kept trying to remember; it might have been Jack, but he wouldn't call him that because he wasn't sure. Sometimes they went drinking. Or sometimes they went down to the Mississippi where they took stones and tried to throw them across. They bet money on who was stronger and the window dresser could throw almost as far as my father, both reaching to the middle of the river. My father described the Big Muddy to me, how deep it was, how wide and opaque, and I imagined they were very strong, to throw stones almost halfway.

It was Christmas Eve, just before closing time, when my father received the telegram from the New York office of J. W. Wenchel's which read, 'Fire the window dresser.' That was all. Just after the Depression, you did what the New York office said. My father emptied the register, giving what money there was to the window dresser. Together they walked out of the store. It was a beautiful winter night and a light snow fell. They bought a bottle of brandy, sharing it as they walked in the snow. Then my father, who was invited somewhere, had to go. He thrust the brandy bottle into the window dresser's hand, leaving him alone. The streets were a brilliant white and the black man's face seemed set off against all that light.

Once when I was very small, my parents threw me in a laundry basket in the back of the car while a twister chased us down an Indiana highway. For some reason they thought I'd be safe, wedged in the basket. Unable to move, I stared at the broad, flat road and the twister coming from behind while my father, sweat pouring down his neck, jammed the accelerator to the floor. We'd driven through Gary on that trip and I remember the pale yellow and blue-grey smoke as something very beautiful.

Dean took one look at Gary and said he'd rather die than spend the night there. I went to the phone at the Holiday Inn to call Robert, the basketball player, whom I'd been calling from every rest stop, dragging my pouch of change silently around with me.

'You're in Gary – right, sweetheart?' Robert, who knew my father always stuck to his schedules, had memorized our itinerary which my father had typed up and taped to the refrigerator weeks before we left. It was filled with spelling errors. 'You'll be in Hannibal at the *moter loge* on Tuesday, right?' Robert pronounced in accordance with my father's errors and

I pretended not to notice. Once after a basketball game, he tried to correct what I called my father's 'typing errors' with a red pencil and I planted myself between him and the refrigerator to stop him. 'Are you having a great time? Shall I come rescue you?' Just then my father walked through the lobby, obviously looking for me. I crouched down so I wouldn't get caught. Though he only voiced his disapproval of Robert by withdrawing silently into his workshop at home, he would vociferously disapprove of my spending what little money I had to call him. He could not understand what I saw in someone whose only attributes were that he was starting center and the owner of a car. I furrowed deep inside the booth as my father wandered by and longed to see Robert again.

At dinner we had a view of the steel mills while my father lectured on the lot of the steel worker. Banging his fork against his plate, he spoke in dollars and cents about working conditions, hourly wage, contribution to the GNP, union leaders of the past. Since the Depression, he'd managed labor. During the Second World War it was the riveters who, when angry because of strike injunctions, threw less rivets. 'It was like a dance,' my father raised his hand over his head. 'Only they did it in slow motion. From smelter to thrower, from thrower to riveter, they danced slower.' Then he pointed to a wall that didn't have a window but behind the wall were even rows of white frame houses. 'If the workers who live in those houses don't see that smoke, they can give up.'

Dean gazed at the yellow, green, and dark blue smoke which rose from the soaring, scattered chimneys, the chimneys poised like a fantastic pipe organ in a somber gothic church. 'Maybe they should give up,' he mumbled.

It was easy to tell when my father was getting angry. His eyes reddened, his face contracted like a held balloon suddenly released, and he always began with 'Let me let you in on a secret.' But the secret never seemed to be the real one. It wasn't the kind I'd hear when my parents whispered and I'd pressed my ear to their closed door and even then it was difficult to tell what they were saying about the aunt who went out alone after dark or my father's boss who called at all hours of the night, crying into the phone during one of his 'binges.' It was never the kind of secret that someone paid you or made you promise not to tell and it wasn't the kind you kept for a friend, nor was it the wisdom great masters imparted to their disciples. These secrets were about table manners, about how a thank-you note needed to be written, about what people think of you when you're bad.

Now my father began to tell him. 'Let me let you in on a secret, some people have to work for a living,' he shouted. 'That's why you don't like it here. Because here people have to work. Since when have you done a goddamn thing, except sit in front of Leo's and smoke with the other hoodlums?' The table shook as my father gripped its edge with his hands. 'You're a lazy bum and everyone knows it.'

Dean ran his fingers through his slicked hair. 'It just makes me sick, to think people have to live where it's so dirty.'

'Pass the green beans,' my mother interrupted my father who passed the beans without taking his eyes from Dean. She always had the same solution to family fights, which usually took place during the evening meal because it was the only time we were all together. 'Pass the salt,' she said to Grandma, tapping Dean on the arm, motioning for him to get the salt from Grandma. Her solution was to keep things moving across the table, to preserve the semblance of a meal as if that would keep us from taking seriously what was being said.

'You're a good-for-nothing, and would you like to know something, you'll never amount to anything, never.'

'Take it easy, will you, Dad?' Dean folded his arms high across his chest as if warding off blows which never actually came.

'Barbara, pass me the bread; thank you, dear.' And to my father, 'Let's forget it, shall we, dear?'

'I'll forget it all right.' Now he glared toward her. 'No need to get my blood pressure up. Someday you'll all see what I mean, when you have to do something for a living, after I'm gone. You'll see what it is, to keep this family going. And he'll learn, when it's time for him to take care of someone. He'll see how he wasted his time.' My father was the great hero of my embattled childhood and, in his irrational anger, I always viewed him as provoked, misunderstood, or poorly loved. When he said we didn't appreciate him, I was the first to feel terrible and want to make it up to him, but the fact is, his criticisms jabbed like those plastic-headed pins he stuck into his triple-A maps. 'You'll learn. You'll find out the hard way,' he pointed ominously at Dean.

'Don't threaten me,' Dean shouted back, flinging his napkin down and storming out the side door of the motel in the direction of the factories.

'Come back here,' my mother called. 'You come back and finish your dinner.' But Dean was already out of earshot, beginning one of his arduous walks, the kind that took him down the dark streets of Milwaukee, into places where you could dance until it was time to go to work. Dean did work once, when he was suspended from school for a month. From the window I watched him, heading swiftly across the street, hands thrust into his pockets, passing the factory where my father, who could not manage his son, had managed all those steel workers.

'You just keep walking,' my father shouted across the restaurant where residents of Gary, who'd come for the roast beef special, stared. 'Just keep going.' Then, when Dean was out of sight, my father threw down his napkin and went to fix the car. The car didn't need fixing but, when 'in one of his moods,' as my mother referred to these outbursts, or while waiting for one of us to come home, my father rearranged the insides of the car until he found himself with a conglomeration of wires, which only a mechanic could unwind, in the fist of his hand.

My mother looked to the factories and then to the parking lot door. 'If he's got a temper,' she said, picking up her fork to finish her meal, 'it's from his father.'

We picked up a hitchhiker, a sailor from Great Lakes, who was going home to visit his girl near Springfield. Dean hopped in back and the sailor crawled in beside my mother who put her blanket away. When we noticed he had tattoos all over his arms, he took off his shirt so we could see all his markings. He'd been a sailor for four years and had seen the world – Bali, the Philippines, the port of Siam. He told us about rooms of gold and women with diamonds in their noses. The tattoos were in pale colors and there were animals, women, and ships – the only things that mattered, he said.

'I've great respect for anyone who serves his country,' my father said and the sailor patted him on the back. 'I built pontoons and tanks,' my father said after a pause. 'I managed a war plant in Gary.'

'Which war was that, sir?' My father told him it was obviously the Second World War and the sailor laughed, wiping his forehead on his sleeve. 'That was a long time ago, sir.'

'Well, this woman was in the Crimean War.' My father pointed at Grandma who was dozing. She'd never seen the Crimea and she still thought we were going to the Petrified Forest. 'How long ago do you think that was?' The sailor shook his head and said he couldn't imagine how long ago it was. We left him at the Springfield exit and everyone saw him wave good-bye but only Dean and I, because we were still facing backwards, caught his austere, fading, blue-and-white salute.

At the next oasis Dean went to the bathroom to smoke a cigarette and I crept to a pay phone to call Robert who said, 'You're at the oasis on the other side of the Mississippi, right?' When we returned, hamburgers on orange plastic trays were waiting with little plastic knives and spoons. Grandma ate cottage cheese because of her teeth and she mashed it with her fork. We sat at a huge formica table, Dean and I sharing a strawberry shake.

'I bet you didn't know,' my father said suddenly, 'That we're related to Genghis Khan.' Dean and I looked at one another. All we knew was that we'd just crossed the Mississippi into Missouri. And I knew from one glance at that river that my father, let alone a crippled window dresser, couldn't have thrown a stone a quarter of the way across.

His eyes were a yellow-brown and seemed to sparkle in the middle of that dull oasis as he told us about the great Mongolian leader who swept down from the hills of his country, establishing the Tartary Kingdom, and he described the dry, scruffy reaches of Russian steppes with charging Tartars on horseback and the great warrior, Genghis Khan. 'You had a great-grandmother six generations back and she was being chased by the Cossacks who killed her husband.' Dean and I leaned on our elbows to listen better while our mother made a face at him. He raised his hand to his heart. 'I swear this is God's truth.' Our mother nodded, cutting her hamburger in quarters with her plastic knife. 'Your great-grandmother carried an infant in her arms and finally, after running for hours, she came to a house in the middle of nowhere. She knocked and stared at the man who opened the door and after he took one look at her, he said, "Will you help me?" Well, you know that she was the one who was looking for help so naturally she was stunned by this turn of events.' Here he paused. He always paused in his stories at strategic moments for suspense.

Grandma nodded during the pause. 'It's the truth,' she affirmed, sitting like a witness to the jury.

My father went on, 'The man, who had wide, oriental cheeks and slanted eyes, led her into the back bedroom where his own infant lay dying of starvation. His wife had died in childbirth two days before. Your great-grandmother nursed both children through the long winter and when spring came, he asked her to marry him. But he was a Tartar and she was Jewish and she refused unless he converted.'

Dean, in spite of his usual rehearsed apathy, blurted out, 'Well, what happened?'

'Obviously, he converted and they had a son from whom my father was descended. That's why all the boys on our side of the family are born with black and blue marks at the base of their spines. Genghis Khan,' my father continued with a plodding emphasis on his words, 'had to sit far forward in the saddle, taking pressure off the elongated coccyx which pained him badly as he rode. And all his direct male descendants are born with those spots.' It was true. Dean was born with one. 'They go away after a while.' My father gave a nonchalant wave of his hand. Then he smiled and said these spots mark the place where our tails should have been.

The Tom Sawyer Motor Lodge in Hannibal was painted a pale shade of crimson inside and out with a plastic statue of Tom fishing off the roof of the motel into the swimming pool. Becky Thatcher stood beside him, clutching a picnic basket. At the center of the pool, Jim, the fugitive slave, huddled on a raft, staring into the water at the plastic fish Tom had hooked. Huck wasn't anywhere to be seen and my father was disappointed because he'd always considered himself more like Huck than Tom. A kind of orphan waif adventurer. Grandma said, 'He's crazy but certainly not an orphan waif,' as she herself could testify.

At dinner Dean said to me, 'I guess they named you Barbara because you're half barbarian.' For some reason everyone else thought that was very funny. My father slapped him on the back as they started to laugh. My mother brought her napkin to her mouth to hide her giggles. But it was Grandma who roared out of control, tears running down her cheeks as she doubled over in laughter. As she laughed, I saw her teeth. They were white and even as rows of soldiers. When people aged, I knew they lost things. Hair, teeth, memory. But every winter Grandma went to Florida where she stayed, she told us, at the Fountain of Youth which made her invincible and she'd never die. But somehow as they all laughed over my name and I saw her teeth, all I could think of was the stunned and horrified look in my father's eyes after he'd gone half-asleep for a glass of water one night and those teeth tumbled out of his drinking cup, catching him on the lip.

After dinner, Dean and some other boy who I never saw before or again conspired and hurled me into the swimming pool. The water was amazingly cold but, hoping to frighten them, I swam down to Tom's plastic fish. The fish was hard and metallic. Soaking wet, I found the pay phone and called Robert. This time he didn't tell me where I was calling from but instead sounded anxious, in a hurry, as if I'd interrupted something. He was indifferent when I explained that I was related to Genghis Khan and had just been thrown into the pool with Jim, the fugitive slave. 'Uh, huh,' he muttered. 'Look, can we talk a little later?' I heard a basketball bouncing five hundred miles away.

'What's wrong with talking now?' But Robert, like my father, was a secretive man and he wouldn't say any more.

That night I must have dreamt of my great-grandmother. It was cold and I was being chased. In my dreams it's always winter. We lived near Milwaukee on a corner where Lake Michigan turns and the wind, cruising down from the Arctic Circle, first strikes land. In the dream I was trying to skate home after the ice storm. The rest of the dream escapes me. One January it rained where we lived and the rain froze. Every twig, every power line was glazed with ice and when the sun shone, everything sparkled like crystal chandeliers. We skated on the streets and across the lawn. My father took snapshots of us, freezing us against the frozen landscape.

We were leaving the motel in the morning on our way to a tour of Mark Twain's house when a blue Ford swung into the parking lot, horn blasting and a hand waving madly in our direction. My father, who recognized the car before it swung into the parking space, turned and stared at me. 'Is that who I think it is?' Robert emerged with a stubbly beard, wearing a dirty white T-shirt and drooping jeans.

'Surprise,' he called, walking briskly toward us. 'Now you know what the big hurry was last night.'

I would have rushed to him but my father stood in front of me. 'How did he find us?'

'You pinned the itinerary on the icebox.'

'I know, but who encouraged him to come looking for us?' I shook my head for I'd never actually told him to come and find me. Robert, who was slapping Dean on the back and kissing Grandma on the cheek, didn't dare approach me until my father moved out of the way. 'I guess you'd like to see my daughter,' my father said sullenly.

Robert laughed. 'You know I didn't drive nine hours for any

other purpose.' My father put his hands in his pockets and rocked on the balls of his feet. Robert pushed his sandy brown hair from his forehead, the way he always did as if shooing flies. It was a nervous habit but my father considered it a defiant gesture, though he was somewhat awed by the long ape-like arms that seemed to reach to Robert's knees. My father kept rocking and Robert, who towered over us all, began backing away. 'Is that all right with you, sir?'

Later we went down to the Mississippi near the place where my father said he threw stones thirty years ago. We talked two rivermen into letting us ride on their barge for a while and my father stood at the edge of the barge, looking into the opaque waters. My mother and Grandma rolled out a picnic of little egg salad sandwiches. 'A million years,' he said: 'imagine being that old.' Dean, Robert, and I sat at the edge of the barge while he broke into a fair Paul Robeson imitation, his voice deep and reaching across the river, 'He must know something but don't say nothing.'

'Is that Kansas on the other side?' Robert interrupted.

My father stared down at him. 'No, Robert, it's Illinois. You drove through it last night, remember?' Robert shrugged his shoulders. 'C'mon, Rob.' He patted Robert on the back. 'I'll race you across.' The two of them were together now at the edge of the barge. 'On your marks, get set, go.' My father made a wild, flapping motion with his arms.

Robert rose into the air, shaped himself into a rainbow arch and disappeared in the dark, churning waters of the Mississippi River. When he surfaced, he was swimming away from us in a smooth, even freestyle, back to Illinois. I stood, screaming and amazed, as he turned, waved at us and kept swimming. 'I don't believe it,' my father muttered. 'I just don't believe it.' Then, 'Come back here,' he shouted. But Robert kept swimming and my father grew silent. Twice in my life I've been hospitalized for serious falls. Both times when my father entered the hospital room, he stood in the doorway, shaking his head back and forth, saying something like 'tsk, tsk.' That was what he did now.

The rivermen who owned the barge aroused him. 'What are

you doing?' they yelled. They pointed frantically at a steamboat ferry coming around the bend and yelled again about some current that would carry Robert to the Gulf of Mexico.

My father knelt, bracing himself with one hand, and, as if coaxing a kitten on a limb, cupped his hand and motioned for him to swim to us. 'Come on back, son.' Seeing my father on his knees, Robert smiled, hesitated, then turned back. When he reached us, we all extended our hands and dragged him on board. Robert sat, drying in the sun, and my father slumped into a corner, staring at him.

'Are you all right, Mr. Miles?' Robert watched my father shake his head back and forth.

As my family climbed the hill, heading back to the motel, Robert caught me by the arm and dragged me silently back to the docks. When I protested, he motioned for me to be quiet. 'You're all wet,' I said.

He pulled me behind a fisherman's shack. 'He tried to drown me. He wanted me to drown. I did it to show him.'

I tried to see where they were on the hill. 'No one thought you'd be so stupid.'

'It's a good thing I'm a great athlete. I wanted to surprise you.'

'By jumping into the Mississippi?'

'No, by driving to see you. I thought you'd be glad.'

I tried to decide whether I was glad to see him or not. A week ago, even a day, I would have done anything to see him but now this unexpected arrival, this surprise, embarrassed me and now I wanted the very thing I'd hoped for to go away. 'You just should have asked if it would be all right,' I said.

'You don't understand, do you? Your father wanted me to drown.'

'No one thought you'd be so dumb.' He tried to pull me to him to kiss me but I wiggled away, not wanting my whole family to see the wet imprint of Robert's body against mine. Instead we kissed delicately on the lips without touching any-where else, then dashed to the top of the hill where my father was turning around in circles like a search light. 'Robert wanted to throw stones,' I breathlessly explained to him, 'the way you did.'

When we got back to our rooms, my mother and Grandma went to take naps. Before disappearing into her room, my mother pulled me aside. 'Don't pay any attention to him,' she said. 'My father was ten times as bad. He locked me in the cellar when your father came to get me and told him I'd gone out with someone else.' Dean and Robert stretched out by the pool. From the lobby of the motel, I saw my father heading across the parking lot and when I called to him, he signaled for me to come along. He was going back to his old stomping grounds. The street he'd lived on, the Muddy River Tavern, Donahue's, J. W. Wenchel's. We walked down a garbage-lined street where he said he used to live. The odor of pizza wafted our way as he scanned the rows of decrepit brownstones; he pointed to a dingy window four stories above with a tattered yellow shade.

'That's where I lived. It used to be a beautiful building.' And, as we passed a bar, 'That's where I used to pick up a little extra money, playing on weekends when I lived here. If Dad hadn't gone broke in the dry goods store, I'd probably still be making money that way.' We walked silently past rundown taverns, past houses of friends who didn't live there any more.

In my mind we were having a conversation. I was asking him if he wanted Robert to drown and if it was true about Genghis Khan. He was laughing and saying of course he didn't want 'poor, dumb Robert' to drown and that the story about Genghis Khan was mostly true, except for where he'd made it better. 'Robert's all right,' I was hearing him say, but I was too young to spend so much time with a man who owned a car, even just a sixteen-year-old man. But all I was really able to bring myself to say to him in words as we walked down the grey streets was, 'I think Robert will drive back tomorrow.'

'Do whatever makes you happy, dear,' he said as he stopped in front of the huge department store. 'Well, at least something's improved around here.' Hands thrust into his pockets, he stared at J. W. Wenchel's department store. It was much bigger now. It had more windows, revolving doors, an annex, a sporting goods section. He could tell this before we set foot inside. We spun through the revolving doors and walked among the long racks of polyesters. We examined the lawn chairs in the garden section, fabric in the yard goods department. 'Good layout,' my father said. 'Good circulation space.' We wandered the circumference of the store from window to window. All the mannequins were dressed for summer. They were on outings with campers and fishing gear. They wore khaki shorts and had dogs with them. We passed each display, absorbing how unreal families appeared during their vacation, until we came to a window curtained with a dull brown sheet. For a long moment my father stared at that sheet, his eyes wrinkled in thought, the way he looked when he was trying to remember if he left the gas on.

Then a hand appeared, pulling at the side of the curtain. It was a black hand and it hooked around into a claw. The curtain came all the way back and a black man, hunched over, with pure white hair, stood in front of us. My father stood perfectly still as the man braced himself and climbed down from the window. To my surprise he was rather tall and not nearly so grotesque as he'd become in my imagination over the years. I tugged at my father's arm but still he didn't move as the man pulled past us, then suddenly came to a halt. 'Mr. Miles,' the window dresser said, 'I knew you'd come back.' My father stared at the man without showing any sign of recognition. 'I knew you'd come back, Mr. Miles.' The man came toward us, extending his good hand. 'They let me have my job again. I always wanted you to know that. They let me have my job.'

'I'm sorry,' my father said, 'but there must be some mistake. He backed up as if seeing his own ghost, aged overnight in a distortion mirror. He paled and stepped away as the window dresser stared at us in disbelief, continuing to extend his hand. My father clutched my arm and dragged me halfway across the store.

Then my father stopped, sighed deeply, and said, 'Wait for me here.' He crossed the store and as he approached the window dresser extended his good hand again. For a few minutes the two men huddled together. Then my father returned, looking drained, and spoke as if to himself. 'Jack,' he said, 'his name is Jack.' Then, remembering I was with him, he spoke with great seriousness. 'Can you find your way to the motel?' I nodded with equal seriousness. Then he took me by the arm, leading me across the store. 'Barbara, this is Jack. Jack, Barbara.' I liked his eyes. I liked the way he shook my hand. And the way he didn't ask where I got my eyes or comment on my being a big girl. He just said, 'I'm pleased to meet you, Miss.' And that was all.

'I'll be back for dinner,' my father called as I began to walk away. 'Tell Mother to wait.'

When he didn't come for dinner, we ate without him. Dean moved the food around on his plate, got up, went to the window, then sat down and moved the food around his plate. Robert and I played Scrabble after dinner but none of my letters made words. Dean couldn't stay away from the window and kept his nose pressed to the glass. 'We should look for him,' he said over and over. 'What if he's hurt? Or just wandering around? We can't let him wander around all night.' He paced back and forth and in his eyes and in his words was that same frightened tone my father always had when Dean failed to come home.

Only our mother was amazingly calm, watching a mystery on television. She loved mysteries. She was always disappointed when she learned who did it and why and much preferred stories that just kept going, week after week, in spiraling plots. 'There are things about your father you don't know,' she said to Dean. 'He can sleep in a tree.' But Dean paced the room and stood in front of the television so my mother had to dodge her head to see.

'How can you just sit there?' he blasted. 'How can you do nothing?'

Dean was halfway across the parking lot when I caught up with him. He didn't say anything to me but let me follow at his side. He went to the car and tried opening the door with a paperclip. Then he gave up and jimmied the hood, trying to move the wires around. Our father had the only set of keys with him. 'Let's walk,' Dean said, slamming the hood down. We went down by the docks where we'd been that afternoon but they were deserted, except for a few fishermen sleeping in their shacks. Then we went up toward the old neighborhood, the brownstones that were now tenements, the department store that was three times bigger than it had been. The streets were grim and empty as we made our way past all the landmarks I could recall from our walk earlier in the day.

For the fifth time, Dean made me repeat exactly what had taken place at the department store. 'Was he afraid? I mean, what did he do? Can't you remember anything?' I was beginning to be more concerned for my brother than for my father and, assuming my mother's veneer of calm, I urged Dean to take it easy.

'He's all right,' I patted him on the arm. 'He just went drinking.'

Dean glared at me, appalled. 'Since when have you known him to go drinking? For a drink, maybe, but drinking, no.' We wandered along the darkened streets. Dean walked ahead, hands in his pockets, except when a car drove by and then he grabbed me and plastered me to the nearest wall and I thought he'd kill me protecting me.

We gave up and went back to the motel. Robert, who followed us to Kansas City like a police escort and would have continued to the Grand Canyon if his mother and mine hadn't conspired to bring him home, dribbled his basketball along the asphalt of the parking lot. When he noticed us walking toward him, he made the ball slide off his shoulders, swirl around his legs in figure eights. In the moonlight, he hurled and dunked into the invisible basket on the motel's west wall.

Grandma was sitting up in bed when I came into the room. Her white hair flowed against the white pillow cases and the lace from her nightgown draped over her once graceful shoulders. 'There's an evil spirit in this family,' she mumbled, spitting three times in the air to chase it away. 'Just like his father,' she said, rolling over to go to sleep. At night I had trouble sleeping because Grandma, who'd lived with us since I was born, whimpered for my grandfather. The only thing I knew about him was he had a canary that never sang again after the day he died.

When I woke, it was still night but I heard a sound coming from the lobby below. I tiptoed down the stairs. One hand played melody on the piano and the other tapped out rhythm on the side. The room was pitch-black, except for the light from the doorway. My father was at the piano, beer cans lined up along the top, the way I imagined them lined up back in the twenties when he earned his living this way.

There were potted palms at the entrance to the room and I decided to duck behind them for a better view. I moved quickly so my father wouldn't see me but as soon as I thought I was safe, I stifled a gasp. From the corner of my eye I saw someone else. A boy stood beside me, also hiding behind the potted palms. Turning slowly, I saw the felt hat, the baggy pants, the knife in hand. The eyes were opened wide and together from behind the palms, Huck Finn's statue and I watched my father, who just kept playing the old tunes I'd never learn to recognize, humming along.

Couples seemed to rise from the shadows, clinging to one another in their desperate dance, then disappearing back to the empty chairs from where they'd arisen while my father smiled and sang to himself. Maybe he was trying to tell me something now in these strange songs which bore no resemblance to what they had been, things he couldn't put in words, about how we all go this way. I wanted to rush to him, to tell him that whatever it was, I think I already knew, but instead I found myself standing perfectly still, unable to move, shaking my head back and forth as I watched my father, a solitary warrior from some fierce race, play.

Idaho As It Seemed

❧ ❧

I REMEMBER CLEARLY. A silver train winding through the mountains as it had through the cities and the plains. The first mountain was stark white against a lavender sky and it was in the distance so we could barely see it. But when we woke, it was outside, the first thing we saw, slipping away, and our mother, capping our amazement, said, 'That's a mountain.' Do you remember the first time you ever saw anything? A horse, a school, a stranger on the road. I don't, but I remember that mountain.

Soon it was behind us. We saw a hundred mountains that day and would see a hundred more each day that followed. Soon a mountain would be like a tree or a lake or anything we've grown used to, but I still can see that solitary white rock, disrupting a very flat plain. By the time we were out of those mountains, the sky had turned crimson, with black clouds like strips of cloth across the sky, and I wasn't sleepy any more and my brother, who was always sleepy, stared wide-eyed at the crimson sky and watched some of the black strips as they cut the mountains in half. Our father said nothing, rarely did. He just looked out the window and our mother packed. It was a beautiful train. It had more windows than any train I've ever seen and it even had windows on the roof so you could lie back and stare at the sky or the gulch when the train passed through.

Memory distorts. There are things I remember quite clearly,

though my brother insists they never happened. For instance, I have a recollection of my mother in a chauffeured limousine, wearing a cool, blue dress, taking my brother to the hospital. Everyone has pointed out to me that it wouldn't make sense to drive a brother who's stopped breathing to the hospital in a limousine and of course they rushed him in an ambulance in the middle of the night. What they insist I remember is the time our parents went to Williamsburg and my father drove. This makes sense, but it's not what I remember.

And then on the train I know our father heaved a deep sigh at the sight of the rising sun. It wasn't a sigh of awe or even fatigue. It was more the kind he'd heave standing in line for a movie or waiting for our mother to finish dressing when they were late. I remember this one, though, because there wasn't anything to wait for; we were on a train going to a specific place. Then she turned to him. She had yellow hair, very bright yellow, and cat's eyes, almost yellow-brown. And she turned to him and shook her head. Then she turned back, away from us all, with a dim look in her eyes, a tooth biting into her lip. On the bed, she'd laid out our clothes, a pile for each of us, and she'd folded everything perfectly, the way she always did, and the train was moving swiftly and the sun had finally risen. Then our father must have forgotten about his sigh and whatever it was that bothered him because he began pointing out the window. He told us what sage brush was and prairie dogs.

The journey, I knew, had begun somewhere. In the back alleys of a city where drunken men lay on the ground, which my mother called Skid Row, and where train tracks extended themselves in all directions like the spokes of a wheel. Each train had a name, not like airplanes which only had numbers. There was the Denver Zephyr, the Wolverine, the City of New Orleans, the Twentieth Century Limited, and our train, the Great Northern. Airplanes don't have the mystery, the endless possibilities, of trains. A train can stop in the middle of nowhere and not be on time. The Great Northern to me was a maze, as twisted and upsetting as my fears.

My fears were what I kept to myself, but beneath an outward

appearance of complacency, there lurked these things that frightened me. I was afraid of the cold and of falling down, afraid of being ambushed on my way home from school. I was afraid of thorn bushes, crawling insects, rabbit's feet, baseball, and a boy at school who meant me no harm. I wasn't afraid of animals. I would have walked into a tiger's cage if anyone let me. Only later would I have nightmares about tigers. I guarded these things silently and seemed very brave.

All this baggage I carried with me. My brother, to my knowledge, wasn't afraid of anything, except me.

The bus was waiting. I don't remember Boise but I remember that bus. We were going to Sun Valley. That was years before Sun Valley was Sun Valley. Before Jackie Kennedy or the movie stars discovered it. Or maybe they had, but I was too young to know about rich people and poor people. I didn't know if we were rich or poor and I didn't care. I knew I was comfortable, that the porter on the train said I was beautiful like my mother, and that I'd never been hungry. My brother had never been hungry either, though he always said he was. He ate whatever he could get his hands on. He was much younger and perhaps I was more aware of his shortcomings while tending to overlook my own. My brother was dark, like a mulatto. Everyone thought it was a joke that we were brother and sister since it seemed we couldn't come from the same race. I treated him accordingly; he was my slave. I wouldn't learn to love him until years later, when things were going his way.

The bus climbed slowly through the mountains. It was morning now and our ears popped as we climbed. Our mother closed her eyes and dozed and when I woke her, our father looked away as if he were to blame. The sun appeared between the mountaintops like a spy and we rode for what seemed hours until finally the bus pushed in the middle of nowhere. We were in a valley and it took me a moment to see, hidden deep in the valley, the lights of what seemed like an Alpine village. It was tucked in the mountains, little flickers from inside the windows of lodges, inns, and small cottages, a tiny wooden village.

Everyone is a creature of habit. It begins with feeding schedules and ends with appointment calendars. I quickly found my way about this place and soon had my routine established, dividing my free time between two activities. Our parents insisted we learn to swim in the turquoise pool, skate on ice that somehow stayed frozen, shoot arrows into distant targets, and eat three square meals a day. But mainly I did this. In the mornings I fed the ducks with crusts of stale bread Betty saved for me in the kitchen, and in the afternoons I went to the stable and Hawk taught me to ride. My brother was always with me. He couldn't do anything without me.

I gave him the small crusts of bread and kept the big ones for myself. We ground the bread against a tree that hung over the pond and the crumbs fell into the water and the ducks pecked at them at our feet. There were six ducks which we named Simon, Ducky, Decoy (who had an arrowhead imbedded in his side, the result of an archer's prank), Angel, Backbone, and Jack Webb (our father named this one). There was definitely no way of telling any of them apart, except for Decoy, because of the hole in his side, but we spent hours arguing about who was who. My brother rode a fat pony named Dumpling. I was given the golden palomino, Pal. Because my hair was long and blond, Hawk called me Pal. 'Hey, Pal,' he'd say, 'tighten up on those reins.' I was vain and foolish and laughed because everyone thought he was talking to the horse. My brother kept behind me.

Hawk told our father he wanted to take us on a long ride into the mountains and our father shook his head but he knew he couldn't do anything about it. He would have gone with us, except he had a fine sliver in a disc somewhere in his spine. Our mother was afraid of horses. She was afraid of everything. She was even afraid to sit in the sun because of her skin. The night before we were going to ride out of the ring for the first time, I remember her pacing the room in a pink gown. The door between the two rooms was open and I saw our father, coming up behind her. He clasped her around the shoulders. But I saw her take his hands off her and push him away.

They were surrounded by people. From the first day they

knew everyone and had a million friends. A wealth of friends to do things with. They knew everyone by name – the guests, the people who served the guests. Late at night I'd hear them whispering about whose marriage was falling apart, whose child had a reading problem, which waitress looked pregnant. There was a man from Norway, named Leif Erikson, which our mother thought was very funny, and he taught us how to swim. My brother dogpaddled around while Leif kept a hand under his belly. Our mother sat in the shade by the pool while we had our lessons and she talked and talked. She smiled and laughed and sometimes she bent forward and was serious. The women confided everything in her. She patted their children and drank the drinks husbands brought her, She always had stories to tell. She'd been a dancer and had seen many cities. But she always came back to my father whom she'd grown up with in Kankakee. Sometimes she listened. She sat quietly and listened to what the other women said. Our father played tennis. Everyone asked him to play and he played all day long. Once they had a fight because she wanted him to come with her into town and help her buy an Indian rug, but he said he'd promised people he'd play tennis with them. While he played, the women told her their problems. Some of them, she said, had had terrible things happen in their lives. Our father was dark, like my brother, and had strong arms and everywhere he went, everyone said what a beautiful man he was. How beautiful they were together. In the evening, when they sat on the patio, sipping from long, icy glasses, they always had people around them.

Hawk lived on the outskirts of Ketchum in what he said was a stupid trailer with beer cans all over the place and he wouldn't let anyone see it. He'd been in the war, in the ocean near Japan, and when he walked he favored his left leg. I didn't know what war was, except I'd seen one movie in my life and it was about war. The film was in brown and white and two ships were firing at each other. There were enormous explosions, brown smoke, small figures falling over the side, and they took me home before the end. When I told him about it, Hawk said war was something like the movie. He knew Hemingway but we didn't know who he was so we weren't impressed. But our mother knew. She asked questions which made us suspect she knew Hemingway in some secret way. She asked about his beard and his work habits, about his wife and his children. She asked if he was as mean as everyone said. When she talked to Hawk, she stood close to him and spoke softly. I remember wondering how it was that she'd gotten to know Hemingway so well. She even knew what prizes he had won. When our father won the tennis tournament, she said that was a good prize too. She made everyone feel better. She had something good to say about everyone and had nothing to hide. Our father never told her secrets because she always told.

The afternoon we rode the trails for the first time, Pal tried to kick me. It was my fault because I walked behind him when I went into the stable, and I knew better. My father saw. He screamed at Hawk. 'You've got a lot of nerve,' he shouted, 'not watching those kids. You're paid to watch those kids.' The hoof only grazed my arm and left a thin red cut but I screamed. My father yelled at the stablehands, at Hawk, at all the horses in the barn. He said he'd have their jobs and the whole damn stable if one hair on our heads was harmed.

Most afternoons we rode in the ring. Rode around in circles. Hawk told us everything. He told us things he probably shouldn't have told. He liked women, liked them a lot. He liked our mother and he would have liked to take her into town because we told him our father played tennis all day long. He was always chewing on something. Gum, pencils, tobacco. He wore jeans, a flannel shirt, boots, and a cowboy hat. Every day he dressed the same and stared at women who came to the stable. He preferred me to my brother. One night we sneaked into a dance and saw Hawk standing on the porch but he didn't see us. He wore blue slacks, a shirt with embroidered flowers, and a string tie. He was almost silly, leaning dressed like that against the railing, his hips pushed forward. Betty was there. She had fuzzy, brown hair and wrinkled skin from too much sun. Even though she was thin, her arms were wrinkled too and we didn't believe it when our father said Betty and our mother were the same age. She wore a long, wide skirt and a thin, white blouse and she leaned on the railing next to Hawk. He slipped his arm around her waist and danced with her on the porch. He kept his hand very low on her back and kept pushing her against him.

The day after we went to the dance we went on our big ride. We'd been preparing for it since Hawk said we were good enough for the trails. Hawk led the way on his chestnut mare, then me on Pal, then my brother on poor Dumpling. Our father stood back and shook his head. We were going to the other side of the mountain and would be gone for the whole day. He waved sadly as if we were going away for a very long time. We rode up a winding hill across the prairie. The sun was warm and shimmered on the marigolds and blue thistle. We didn't know our mother was back in the room, arranging our clothes, or that our father was feeding the ducks crusts Betty had given him. For some reason it never occurred to us that we would ever leave this place.

We rode to an Indian village on the outskirts of town and two Indians made us lunch. They lived in shacks and had very wrinkled faces. We didn't know our father had given Hawk money to pay them to feed us cornbread and some kind of roasted meat, potatoes cooked in the fire and fresh milk. While resting on the ground, under a tree, Hawk tossed in his sleep and he opened his mouth when he lay on his side. One of the Indians gave me a beaded pouch and my brother an arrowhead which I put in the pouch and lost on the way back down the mountain. During the ride back through town, a man with a grey beard passed us and went into a store and Hawk said that was Hemingway.

There are few pure moments. Moments that come out clean and you carry them away with you as they were. There are moments I see clearly as if they were taking place right now. They are like a familiar face. There was the eagle in the lower branches of the tree, the magician with the failed tricks, the painting in our living room with the procession of hidden faces and the painter who killed herself because of it. And much later, that first dance in a dimly lit room between skinny arms. I'll always know these the way I know that ride down the mountain. Our parents were at the stable when we returned. They were smiling. They had tanned faces and sharp eyes. Our mother wore lavender like the mountains and this time she stood out. We really saw her. He wore pale blue slacks and an open white shirt and his arm was on her shoulder. I never saw anything so complete, so perfect, as they were then and they even knew to meet us at six sharp.

They said in the morning the bus would take us to the train. Our father gave us the crusts he hadn't fed to the ducks but I told him to keep them. My brother, who always followed my example, also refused. When we returned to our rooms, we left the bag with the crusts on the window sill. That night we watched our parents dance. She wore a long, lime-colored dress and he wore a dark suit. They danced slowly in each other's arms and clapped when the music stopped. They never seemed to look at one another. We watched until they carried us upstairs.

As I slept, I thought I was walking on a road and I heard the sound of a bicycle behind me. I walked faster but the bicycle also came faster and it was dusk when I reached the place where I had to cross the field. My father had told me about the redwoods, giant ruddy trees that loomed like mountains. The boy dragged me into a forest of redwoods and I was like a dwarf and not as beautiful as I'd been. He pushed me deep into the woods but didn't really harm me. He just left me there. When I woke, my brother slept and our parents hadn't returned. I saw empty beds and went downstairs. I listened as our father played 'Small World,' 'Summertime,' and 'Funny Valentine' on the piano with a swing bass and my mother sang and there was a crowd of people around. Then I saw this, through the door that was ajar. Our mother seemed to drop back, disappear. She stared at our father who played and then slowly she slipped away.

But he didn't even seem to notice or mind. He just kept playing and everyone else stood around him. He always had a crowd when he played. Something made me sad, about my mother going away and my father not noticing, but he seemed very happy so I was sure it was all right with him. She never did anything without first asking if he minded. She walked out onto the patio, passing the stairs where I now sat crouched and I could see that she was sad the way I was. It was very dark on the stairs so she couldn't see where I was. She leaned against the patio wall. The wind blew at her lime-green skirts and she breathed deeply; she sighed almost the way he'd sighed on the train. She looked out in the direction of the inn and the duck pond and then out of nowhere, it seemed, the man from Norway, Leif, appeared. The stairs where I was crouched, which led up to our rooms, were right between the patio and the room where my father played. There was glass on either side so I could see both my mother and my father from the stairs. She was to my left and he to my right. When Leif came and stood beside my mother, they moved over slightly, almost as if to move closer to me. I heard my mother make a joke about Vikings being stronger, that's how close they were standing. And I heard him tell her the old Viking proverb, 'If it doesn't kill you, it makes you stronger.'

That made her laugh and he started laughing too. I almost laughed with them but I knew that if I did and they heard me, I'd have to go to bed, which I wasn't ready to do. Then Leif spoke in a very loud voice and said he was a real Viking. My mother laughed louder but she also put her fingers to her lips to shush him, the way she did when my brother was asleep. She seemed to become very calm then. She didn't look sad any more the way she had when she walked out onto the patio. They leaned their arms on the railing of the patio, talking so I couldn't hear, and then he said something which made her look very strange. She nodded and took his arm. She let her hand slide on his corduroy jacket. He wore a very nice brown jacket and dark pants and I'd never seen him in anything other than a bathing suit before. They walked to the far side of the patio, behind the stairs, and I couldn't see them any more.

The next thing I knew my father was standing above me. He

was staring down as if he weren't certain of what he saw. He kept asking me over and over what I was doing there as he swooped down and pulled me up into his arms. It was light on the stairs now and I was very cold. His eyes were tired and his beard scratched my cheek. He always had a beard in the morning. He carried me up the stairs slowly, one step at a time, as if he were afraid he'd fall. I looked around but all the other people were gone and as he held me my father moved his fingers back and forth against my side because they ached from playing all night.

I told him about waking up because of the forest and the boy and he said I shouldn't have stayed on the stairs because I could catch cold. He blew his breath on my hands to warm them. Then he held me very close and told me I should forget whatever it was I thought I saw.

Foolish Pleasure

GERALD SITS IN THE middle of the bed, propped up by three of Vera's throw pillows. There is no light on in the room, except for the blue-gray rays of the television that make their faces appear as if they were watching by candlelight. Vera wishes it were candlelight. Around his neck Gerald wears a pair of binoculars. When each race begins, he raises the binoculars to his eyes to watch because this makes him feel that he is actually at the track. Vera sits beside him, holding a bowl of popcorn. She has put too much butter on the popcorn and the morsels are soggy. Gerald has commented that it is a good thing Nathan is not with them. If Nathan were here, he would look at all that butter and give them an hour-long lecture on cholesterol.

Nathan is Gerald's best friend; he is a cardiologist and he lives three blocks away. Gerald is an orthopedic surgeon who has been living with Vera in her apartment for the past five months. Hearts and bones. These are the two topics of conversation that most preoccupy Nathan and Gerald when they are together. And racehorses. It was Nathan who called Gerald an hour ago when they had just settled down to dinner to remind him about the race. Vera believes that, because Gerald is a medical doctor, he must be an entirely responsible human being, never frivolous. She finds his interest in racehorses to be a basic paradox, the only paradox in Gerald's character. Gerald has had to convince Vera several times that her attitude toward medical doctors is pure mythology and that his interest in race-horses is purely aesthetic. This must be true, Vera tells herself, as Gerald puts his binoculars to his eyes and reaches for another handful of popcorn, because he never bets.

'A racehorse is a precision machine,' he has said to her. 'There's more going on inside a horse's fetlock than inside most people's brains.' With this Vera must agree, even though she has little or no knowledge of what actually does happen inside a fetlock. In fact, she referred to that part of a horse as 'ankle' until Gerald corrected her. Vera does not like being together with Nathan and Gerald because of the amount of time they spend hypothetically betting odds on racehorses on the basis of their physiology. Nathan knows the blood pressure of every major racehorse, living or dead, before and after a race. This is no mean accomplishment. Nathan claims that racehorses have cardiac arrests, just like people. Gerald knows about joints and he makes predictions on the basis of X rays. Once he predicted that a certain horse would shatter a pelvic bone within the next month. Three races later the horse broke down. While Vera believes that all of this is a waste of time, she finds it striking that often when they do these predictions they are correct. She is also impressed that they never do them for money. They, on the other hand, see nothing miraculous in any of this. 'We make predictions all day long that cost someone a lot of money,' they say.

Gerald has been relatively quiet all evening, except for a request that they do not eat out and a few comments about the race they are watching from Belmont. Vera has grown accustomed to the fact that they will often spend their evenings together watching reruns, but she has not gotten used to Gerald's reticence. When she lived with Michael, her ex-husband, he talked a blue streak unless they were fighting, in which case he never uttered a word, sometimes for days. Gerald is the opposite. Except for one or two explosions a week, he is silent. It is certainly a more relaxed way to live. It is also duller. When she was married to Michael, she never believed that one could live in the same apartment with a man and feel as lonely as if one lived alone. Now she believes that only that is possible.

'Remember that boy I told you about? The one who broke his leg in a motorcycle accident in New Hampshire? The one who kept asking when he was going home?'

'The one whose leg was set in that small hospital in Vermont and then an infection set in and he was rushed to Manhattan. To you.'

Gerald nods. She can tell that he is pleased that she recalls the details of the case because it assures him that she listens. It is important to a man who rarely speaks to know that some-one is listening when he does.

'Nathan diagnosed an arterial stoppage. Right here.' He points to a place somewhere high on his thigh. Vera asks if that means it was not an infection, and Gerald says it was not an infection. He removes his glasses and the binoculars and puts them on the bed stand. She thinks suddenly that he looks foolish in those binoculars. 'Gangrene,' he says in a voice so soft she can hardly hear. 'I haven't seen anything like it since the war. The whole leg was gray when we sawed the cast off.' He shakes his head back and forth and tells her that they had to amputate, that the patient was only seventeen, that he told Gerald he would hate him until the day he died. 'But he stopped asking when he was going home,' Gerald says with a sigh, almost of relief.

Creeping along the covers of the bed, Gerald's hand finds its way to Vera's and they clasp tightly. She places the bowl of popcorn on the bed stand beside her. Gerald takes her hand and presses it closely to his face. 'So frail,' he mutters over and over again. 'So frail.' He looks at her hand as if he were counting the bones, naming them. Once he made her lie still so that he could name all the bones in her body, which he had not done since medical school, just to see if he still could.

'I'm glad that I don't have to make those kinds of decisions about other people's lives.'

'Sometimes you make such decisions,' Gerald says, unwilling to be the only one with such a burden. Vera shakes her head and recites to him the old nursery rhyme about sticks and stones breaking bones but names never hurting. Vera is a graphic artist who works in the production department of a national magazine. Part of her day is spent mailing back artists' portfolios.

She pulls her hand abruptly away. For some reason she is frightened by Gerald's examining it so conscientiously. What if he were to see something wrong? That tiny paper cut turning gray. The spot of blood where she bit a hangnail away. If she lost her hand, she could not work. If she could not work, she would hate him.

'What's wrong?' he asks, surprised by the abruptness of her gesture.

'Nothing,' she says, tossing her head back with a laugh. 'Come on, let's do the dishes and go to bed.'

Later that night, Vera lies beside Gerald, leaning on her elbow, watching him sleep. Gerald, as a medical doctor and as a generally exhausted man, is one of those people who seem always able to find their sleep. Vera, who Gerald says has the jittery temperament of the finest racehorses, has to fight for snatches of sleep during the night. The slightest noise will keep her awake for hours; the slightest flash of a thought or the recollection of a fear leads to more thoughts, more fears. 'Every night for me is a thousand and one,' she has said.

In the moonlight, Gerald's face appears white, ghostly to her, and his radiant blue eyes are closed. His hair, she thinks, daring to reach out and touch it, is like fleece – priceless and golden, something sought after but never attained. But it was the eyes that first captured her. The night they met, Vera was sitting on the corner of Broadway and Seventy-ninth Street. She had placed a jacket over a dog that had just been hit by a car and the dog staggered, dressed in her jacket. Gerald walked by. He was tired. He had worked a double shift in his residency at St. Luke's; he had not slept in thirty-six hours and he was now going home to do just that, because in eight more hours he had to do his rounds at the hospital. The last thing he needed to concern himself with was an injured dog. But it was the woman he noticed, he told her later. She seemed as crumpled and helpless as the animal she was protecting. 'I'm a doctor,' he said, bending down and removing the jacket. He made the dog lie down. He saw that the dog was not bleeding and gently pressed his fingers into its spine, along the curve of its legs. 'The dog's hip,' he muttered after the brief examination and Vera burst out laughing.

'The dog is hip,' she said. 'Get it?' Her laughter must have seemed semihysterical at the time over something that was clearly not funny, but then, as she explained to Gerald later that evening (after they had bandaged Broadway, the name they gave the dog), 'My husband left me this afternoon. For a ballerina who can spin on her toes in twenty-seven circles without stopping. He told me that. Can you imagine?'

As she watches Gerald sleeping, it is apparent to her that he will not be staying much longer. The men who plan to stay with a woman are restless when they sleep; they need arms to secure them in the night. Gerald only needs whatever sleep he can snatch before he is due in surgery in the morning. Still, she thinks, as she reaches out across the pillow, his hair is like fleece. She touches it gently, and it is soft against her hand and very golden in the moonlight. She leans forward.

He is muttering something in his sleep and he has never done that before. She leans closer, still touching his hair and putting her ear close to his mouth. It is a name but she cannot quite make it out. It begins with an 'R' like Roni or Roberta. In his sleep, Gerald is comforting someone she does not know and all she can feel is a surge of jealousy. She turns back onto her side away from him. He mutters the name again, and she buries her face in the pillow. It will not be until weeks later, after Gerald has moved out, that she will learn, through a casual mention by Nathan, that it is the name of the boy whose leg Gerald cut off the previous afternoon.

It is a week later when Vera meets Michael for lunch in the park. It is a clear afternoon in May and they decide to picnic.

Though Michael has willingly become Vera's best friend and confidant, Vera is not at all certain she likes him in this role. But she is certain that it is all she can have from Michael for the moment. She takes his arm as they walk. 'I can't explain it, but he's never there. He's always dashing somewhere. And even when he's standing still, it's just to rest so he can run off again.' Michael and Vera now have two topics of conversation - Sami, Michael's ballerina with whom he is relatively happy, though they rarely see one another because of her rigorous schedule, and Gerald. When they were married, they had many more topics of conversation. Vera is afraid that they are drifting apart.

'He has many responsibilities.' Michael offers the only solution he can think of. It is not the explanation Vera wants. She knows all about Gerald's responsibilities.

'I don't even know if I like him,' Vera sighs, tightening her grip on Michael's elbow.

'That's much more serious, then.' Michael shakes his head as they walk forward in solemnity. They find a spot near the reservoir beneath an arching maple and a dogwood in bloom and flop down beside one another, their shoulders barely touching. A luminous pink frisbee sails across the bushes just past them and falls at the feet of a girl as she reaches out to catch it.

'Maybe we should get back together, give it another try,' Vera suggests, rather wistfully, wondering if Michael will take her seriously.

'Us?' Michael asks, unwrapping a baloney sandwich from the picnic Vera has packed. 'I'll never regret having married you.' Michael strokes her hand, trying to make her feel better. 'We've learned a great deal from one another.'

Vera nods. She knows this is true. She met Michael at a convention for graphic artists where they worked for companies whose booths were side by side. Vera's sketches were all from her illustrated children's books. They consisted of fiery dragons with green scales and princesses stranded in castles. Michael's were more modern; he drew pages filled with colored squares. Only a month after they met, Michael was drawing squares with eyes and mouths and she was drawing princesses in three dimensions, cut in halves, eyes gazing up and down at the same time. They both lost their jobs. While collecting unemployment, they had gotten to know one another.

'I think he's going to leave me,' Vera says, her voice quavering.

'Why should he leave you? Michael asks, trying to remember exactly why he left.

'I don't know, but I just know he will. Then what will I do?'

That night Gerald comes home with a deep gash on his left forearm just above the wrist. He explains that he cut himself during a surgical procedure on the cranium of an old woman. He says that he was relieving the pressure to the skull after a fall that led to a contusion. Vera is somewhat revolted. She does not know why but she finds it odd to make love to a man who has cut himself on the bone of another. She wishes she lived with a carpenter who came home with black-and-blue thumbs or a mechanic with grease embedded beneath his nails. She has already eaten and Gerald is tired, so when he sits down, she serves him. While he eats his lamb chops, he picks up the bones with his hands. Vera looks at the gash on his arm and at the bone he gnaws on. She thinks she is losing her mind. As he reaches for the next bone, she sees him lifting the amputated leg of the boy, bringing it to his lips and chomping down. He smiles at her and shreds of meat stick between his teeth. He sits back and chews, then bites hard again and a droplet of grease appears on his chin. The boy now had pneumonia, Gerald told her the day before yesterday. Chewer of corpses, she says to herself, watching Gerald and wondering why she feels that he is eating something out of her as well.

Vera rises and goes into the kitchen. She begins washing the dishes while Gerald continues eating alone. Vera knows that it is so rare for her not to sit with him while he eats that Gerald will feel uneasy. He will not know what to do with his hands or what to think about. He will try not to think dark thoughts of the day. Gerald has confided in Vera that sometimes if he looks in the mirror and he is not wearing his surgical gown, he does not recognize himself. If he is wearing the gown with the name of his hospital emblazoned on the corner pocket and a cap with a mask over his head, he knows exactly who he is and why he does what he does.

Vera is washing the dishes, which are hidden beneath a veil of suds. She is wearing red playtex gloves and the water is steaming hot as it runs over the British china which her mother-in-law gave her when she married Michael, even though she never approved of the marriage. She hears Gerald leave the table and walk to the doorway. She knows he is standing there, watching her, and that his dinner is not entirely finished.

Gerald moves behind her slowly. He comes to the sink and wraps his arms around her waist. He lets his hands wander over her hips, her rib cage, her breasts. She does not stop washing the dishes. He kisses the back of her neck and pulls her away from the sink, turning off the water and leading her into the bedroom. In the bedroom, he takes off her clothes, slowly, one article of clothing at a time, except for the plastic gloves. He does not remove them. 'Doctor Vera,' he says, laughing as he pins her gloved hands to the bed and makes love to her. Finally she pulls the gloves off and flings them across the room.

Three days later Gerald announces that he has found an apartment off Central Park West that is just across the way from the hospital and that Foolish Pleasure won the Kentucky Derby in 1:59, which did not break any track records. He says these two facts in one rapid, run-on sentence, and Vera is too confused to feel hurt immediately. When she finally understands, she asks why, and he replies simply, 'Because it is time.' For some reason she accepts his answer. He has brought few possessions with him, so that his moving is accomplished in a matter of hours. 'I'll call,' he says, kissing her on the brow like an old friend when he leaves. As she closes the door behind him, she is surprised to find that she feels momentarily relieved.

Vera goes to her drawing board in the extra bedroom, which she has converted into a studio. She pins her instructions onto the bulletin board. She prepares her brushes and paints, water and paper, methodically, in even rows in front of her. She stares at the instructions and then reads and rereads the book she is supposed to illustrate. She has two weeks to complete the preliminary sketches or else she will lose her commission. She reads the book for the fifth time. It is the tale of a little girl who lives alone in the woods since her grandfather died. She waits for something to happen, something magical. She believes in miracles. One day she sees a deer, darting through a clearing in the woods. She spots the white tail as it flickers in the sunlight and she follows it until the deer leads her to another cabin hidden in the woods where a man lives with his two children.

Vera cannot do the drawings because she despises the story; it gives children false hopes and teaches them to be optimistic. The editor she works for justifies his decision. 'What's wrong with giving people a little hope these days?' She picks up her brush and begins to paint. She paints foliage in russet and crimson, blood orange and pumpkin, golden yellow and soft scarlet, a touch of sienna and pine green. She works her way slowly toward the cabin. At first she paints it flat and many leveled. It is too modern, so she heightens it and darkens the wood until it appears like a Victorian mansion. She abandons the house and works on the girl. She places her in the doorway with long, blonde hair so that soon she becomes another stranded princess. Vera examines the painting on her board. It is wrong. She has never seen anything so wrong. She pulls it off the board and rips it into as many pieces as she is able.

Broadway is seated by the window, staring across the way at a large black-and-white cat. The two spend most of their days just gazing at one another. The distance is safe for them. Broadway would cower if the cat ever came closer. She pats Broadway on the head, pitying him for his short-lived pleasures. Suddenly he reminds her of Gerald, and she feels a delayed reaction setting in. She backs away from her adopted dog. She goes into the bedroom, which also reminds her of Gerald, flops down, and puts her face into the pillow. She cries and wonders what will ever become of her.

Gerald moved out so quickly that he neglected to call Nathan. That evening when Nathan calls and asks for Gerald, Vera bursts out crying. She explains slowly, through her sobs, what has occurred. As Nathan launches into a pep talk, colored with a series of locker room platitudes ('roll with the punches,' 'stiff upper lip,' 'don't give up the ship'), Vera can only recall the old lessons that go back to her kindergarten years – about what all the king's horses and all the king's men couldn't do any more.

'Nobody ever died of a broken heart,' Nathan says. 'What you need is some fun.'

Vera arrives at Nathan's apartment half an hour later. Her eyes are red and swollen and she is coughing slightly, in the early stages of an upper respiratory infection.

'You look like the last scene of *Camille*,' Nathan says, handing her a bourbon as she walks through his apartment, where she has never been before. On the walls are framed posters from the Buffalo Bill Rodeo in Cody, Wyoming. There are wall hangings of fine leather riding crops, Indian blankets, and an assortment of bridles, one blue ribbon for best-in-show. 'Souvenirs,' Nathan says with a sweep of his hand.

They drive out to Long Beach, where there is an amusement park on the shore. The ocean appears dark, the waves breaking out of the darkness. They ride the roller coaster and Vera thinks she is going to be sick. Nathan buys her cotton candy and a hot dog. 'You'll be just fine,' he says. He takes her to a bump-'em car ride and through a freak show where she sees a man with no arms and legs who rolls on the floor like a seal, a lady with skin like an alligator's hide, and Siamese twins who are also midgets. He takes her to the merry-go-round and they get on horses side by side. While Vera goes up, Nathan goes down. She reaches for the ring in the center but misses. The merry-go-round plays pipe organ music, and its yellow and green lights spin like orbits, flashing on and off in unison. They throw baseballs at dolls with smiling faces, spray water into a gaping mouth that causes a balloon to expand and burst, place quarters in squares that contain geographical locations in New York, trying to win bottles of whiskey. Vera bets the Brooklyn Bridge, Nathan the Statue of Liberty, but the wheel spins to Madison Square Garden twice in a row.

'I'm getting a fever,' Vera says, and he places a hand on her forehead.

'You're just fine,' he says, leading her to the tunnel of love.

Inside the tunnel it is dark and damp, and their boat moves slowly, tipping from side to side. There are deep, hollow sounds that echo, sounds of mysterious animals calling, a Bela Lugosi laugh over the loudspeaker. Something moist and gossamer brushes against her cheek and she trembles. Something wet like a cobweb but with substance like a stiff limb reaches out and grabs her by the arms. She shudders and presses her head against Nathan's shoulder.

When they arrive back at her apartment, she is not well. Nathan touches her brow. 'You do have a fever,' he says. He makes her slip into her pajamas and brings her a tray of hot tea and honey. He pulls the covers over her and takes Broadway for a walk. When he returns, he shouts through the long corridors of her apartment, 'This dog is not leash trained. How can you walk an animal that drags you down the street?' Vera does not answer and Nathan takes Broadway off his leash. The dog bounds into the bedroom and Nathan follows.

Vera is sitting up in bed with Nathan's stethoscope, which she has removed from his bag, pressed to her chest, breathing deeply, then coughing. 'I can't hear anything,' she mutters.

Nathan adjusts the stethoscope to the spot above her heart. 'I swear, Vera, it's only a cold.' Vera hears the steady thud, thump, swish repeated over and over, and she is assured. She is awed by the sound of her own body at work, performing its lifelong chores. For a while she sits, listening to the thud, thump, swish, and it is repetition in which for her there is no monotony. 'See,' Nathan says, 'smooth like a tennis stroke.' He removes the stethoscope from around Vera's neck and places his hand where her heart must be.

Vera and Nathan are driving. They are driving swiftly up the road toward the backwoods of Maine, along the shore drive. They have just taken the road that leads to the house. After seeing Nathan for two weeks, Vera decided that she wanted to go away, to Woodhaven. She said to him, 'Nathan, I want to go home.' He nodded and said he would take a couple days off and that they should see about purchasing whatever supplies they would need. Vera was pleased that she did not have to ask him to drive her but that he offered on his own.

They are driving past rows of winter pines and spruces, junipers and maples. Vera cannot help wishing it were autumn. She would like to show Nathan Woodhaven in autumn. The road narrows around the bend and opens onto the shore. On their left, yellow and gray cliffs jut up against the pale blue sky. On their right is a steep drop to the rocks where the waves crash far below. When she was seven years old, Vera threw her favorite doll over those cliffs and watched it crash against the rocks. She doesn't remember why she did that; it was just after her father died.

They pull up in front of a large wooden ranch house, made out of timber from the surrounding woods and hidden behind a row of pines. Nathan unpacks the car while Vera opens the house, which has been closed for almost a year. He brings the suitcases and cartons of groceries inside while she unlocks the doors and the windows, opening them wide to let the house air. He walks into the middle of the living room, which is dome shaped and two stories high with picture windows on both sides, so that one has a view of both the woods and the ocean but cannot see the land. 'Incredible,' he says as he paces from corner to corner. 'Just incredible.'

While Nathan walks through the living room, studying the joints and hitting beams, Vera spots the glass vase where she kept her seaside discoveries over the years. Pieces of broken bottles made smooth by the sea shimmer as the light refracts through them. Shells, sand dollars, sea horses all suspended between the bits of glass and polished stones. Pale coral and soft yellow shells. The smooth, rounded sand dollars. And the sea horses. It was an unexplained phenomenon, her father told her when they began to find them during that last week in August. Just one week, that year, the current must have shifted, bringing a warm current north until it turned cold and they

were washed to shore, already dead. Most of the sea horses were broken now, their tails dangling a few inches below them in the glass bowl; a few remained intact, large and whole. All were dried and calcified. The trophies from her many walks along the sea as a child with her father.

'Nice shell collection,' Nathan says, tapping the rim of the glass with his fingers. Nathan kicks the floorboards and pounds the studs. Together they go outside and stand at the edge of the cliff. Vera watches the ocean crashing against the rocks below. Nathan takes a fistful of soil and clenches it in his hand. He stomps on the ground. With his eye he measures the angle of descent and the extent to which the house has been cantilevered over the cliff. 'It will fall into the sea in five years,' he says as they walk back to the house.

'No, it won't,' Vera replies. It is their first disagreement but she feels a familiar pattern setting in.

She lights a roaring fire on the hearth, and the living room is illumined, a brilliant orange, by the dancing flames. It is late, near dusk, and outside they can see the sky paling as fingers of pink reach across the clouds. That is a color she remembers, the opalescence. She is preparing a feast for them, piling steaks and chicken thighs on the grill, stuffing ears of corn still in their shucks into the embers. She is chopping onions and tomatoes and peppers. She is slicing mushrooms and fresh pineapple that she will also place on the grill. Wild rice is steaming on the stove. She finds two baskets in a cupboard and sends Nathan outside in the woods to pick the wild strawberries and raspberries that grow around their property at this time of year. They will have them for desert, with fresh cream. He returns just as dinner is ready. He has collected almost a full basket of each. He is amazed that they grow in such abundance.

After dinner, she takes him upstairs. In her room, a small room with pink and white curtains that looks onto the ocean, she takes down a large box from the closet. 'My first drawings,' she says. Nathan opens the box. Inside are crayon sketches, watercolors, and finger paints; pictures of dogs and houses, mothers and fathers and horses, many horses. 'I had an art teacher who was obsessed with horses. She said if you couldn't draw a horse, then you couldn't draw anything. As you see, I never could.'

It is dark outside, but a bright moon shines full on the horizon and the ocean is sheathed with silver, flickering on its surface like glitter. They are tired and crawl into the big bed in her parents' room. Vera sees the whiteness of Nathan's oval face pressed against the pillow, round and bright like the moon that shimmers on the ocean outside. He smiles and she sees his teeth. They are perfectly even.

Vera reaches across the bed but no one is there. Her hand rubs against the cool sheets. She opens her eyes and sunlight streams into the room. Suddenly she sees a pair of legs rising from the floor near the foot of the bed. She hears the sound of a grunt and then a groan. 'C'mon Vera; let's get the old blood circulating.'

Nathan stands up and begins touching his toes. With her hand, she sweeps across the empty spot on the bed, a request for him to join her. He is doing jumping jacks and counting to himself. 'Nathan, it's six-thirty,' she says, glancing at the clock and then pulling the covers over her head.

'C'mon, Vera. We're in the country. You don't want to lie around all day.' Nathan puts on his sneakers and his jogging shorts. He pulls a sweatshirt over his head. He yanks the covers off Vera and drags her out of bed. She goes into the bathroom and throws cold water on her face.

Outside, Nathan claps his hands together like a camp director rounding up his stray campers. He is running in place as she joins him. The morning is damp and there is a low mist over the land. As they begin to run, his muscles are taut and, as he leaps into the air, the tendons on the back of his knees visibly flex. His enthusiasm is stunning. Vera pauses, feigning to tie a shoelace. She turns and walks back toward the house. Nathan, already halfway down the road, jogs back. 'Hey, Vera,' he calls, 'you old lazybones.'

Vera has been working for almost two days straight, without

sleeping. She has not made a single phone call. She has not seen anyone, and when the phone rings, which it often does, she does not answer. Nathan has left several messages with her doorman, which she has not read, though she suspects, from his grin as he delivers them, that the doorman has.

She has been working on the illustrations for the book about the little girl in the woods. On her drawing board she completes the house. It is sturdy and solid. A real house with real trees where a real person could live. As she presses the drawing carefully between two sheets of acetate in her portfolio, the doorbell rings. She glances at the clock. It is one in the morning and they are on time. She has ordered a pizza from the all-night pizzeria around the corner. A medium-size combination with anchovies.

When she opens the door, she sees the pizza extended by two hands. She follows the hands along the arms to the body until she comes to a white coat and the name of a hospital on the breast pocket. She looks up and sees Gerald staring at her. She wonders if times have gotten that bad.

'I ran into the delivery boy in the elevator,' Gerald offers as explanation. 'He recognized me right away. I hope you don't mind. I paid for it. I know you sometimes work late. Are you alone? I don't want to disturb you.' His eyes deepen suddenly and he looks very sad. 'I had to talk to someone.'

She takes the pizza out of Gerald's arms. He looks tired and worn. His skin is sallow and he appears older than she remembers. She glances at his hands, which remain extended, and she no longer sees the trace of a gash on his arm.

'It's terrible, just terrible.' His voice begins to crack. She has never heard Gerald sound so troubled or look so worn before. She leads him inside and pours Coke into two glasses. She finds napkins and opens up the pizza on the kitchen table.

'I'm sorry about the anchovies. I know you don't like them.'

Gerald slumps into a chair, resting his face in his palms. Simultaneously they reach for adjacent slices of pizza, which they are forced to tear away from one another. Broadway comes into the room and lies on the floor, close to Vera.

'Ruffian died,' Gerald says at last, his eyes gazing down.

Vera's head bobs back and forth in acknowledgment, as if she were treading water. She is tired and her thoughts are not entirely clear but she knows who Ruffian is. Ruffian is the boy whose leg was amputated, the name Gerald muttered in his sleep one night before he left her. The boy has died. She feels terrible. She wonders if he hated Gerald as he died, the way he promised he would.

'I just heard it on the radio. I was coming out of surgery. They had to put her to sleep with a large dose of phenobarbital.' Vera is tired but she is not that tired. She knows that they do not put boys to sleep and that Gerald would not have heard about it on the radio. It comes to her slowly as he tells her how he saw Ruffian run on that shattered leg, only heart and instinct left. That she splintered both sesamoid bones and that they protruded at different angles from the back of the fetlock. As he speaks, he bites into his slice of pizza and grease drips down his chin and falls on his clean white jacket. As Vera watches the drop of grease, it comes to her that he is not talking about a boy at all. He is talking about a horse.

'I didn't know who else to talk to. I had to see someone, someone who could understand. You didn't watch? You didn't see the race? Everyone was watching.'

'Honestly, Gerald, I don't even know what day this is. That's awful. It's really awful.' Vera does think it is awful. She also thinks it is awful that he has not called her in the past six weeks since he moved out.

Gerald suggests they watch a rerun of the race on the late news. They go into the bedroom and sit down, propped up by her throw pillows, on the bed. She takes Gerald's binoculars out of the drawer. 'You forgot these.' He shakes his head and gestures for her to put them away. He does not want them. She puts the binoculars around her neck and, as they wait for the race to come on, she adjusts the focus. At first the room is blurred, a progression of shadows, but soon the furniture, the corners, the mirrors all assume their former shape. She looks at Gerald, but he is sitting too close and all she can make out is the skeletal outline of his frame. She turns the binoculars around and he appears small and distant on the bed. A diminutive of his former self. She thinks that she has a homunculus seated on her bed, the kind the ancients believed lived in the sperm and grew to maturity in the womb. She begins to laugh at the thought of a homunculus on her bed and soon her laughter blossoms into near hysterics. Gerald stares at her in wonder. 'You look so silly,' she says, pointing to the binoculars as if they were the source of her laughter.

The horses approach the gate. Vera crosses her legs and leans forward to watch. She drops the binoculars on the side of the bed. For the moment, she forgets about Gerald. She forgets to close the space between them on the bed as she used to do. The gun goes off. The horses are neck and neck with Foolish Pleasure moving ahead by a nose. She sees them running together now in slow motion, lunging forward, racing around the bend. Slowly Ruffian begins to pull back while Foolish Pleasure races out of the frame, running alone toward the unseen finish line. The news camera zooms and holds Ruffian for an instant at a halt, suspended in midair, a stiff leg extended, as if frozen there. Vera sees her stumbling, collecting herself, then stumbling again. She sees into the fetlock. Those three frail bones upon which all the weight rests. The fetlock dropping clear to the ground. The sound of splintering, of bone emerging from behind flesh, like a rubber band snapped and shot across the room. And she wonders about the pain - if she felt much pain.

The Other Moon

SINCE I'VE BEEN LIVING in Cody, which is going on six months, I've been spending my evenings at the Tumbleweed Saloon. The Tumbleweed is one of those places you'll either visit once in your life, like a tourist, and never come back again, or, even if you're a drifter, you'll just keep coming back, night after night, until you get sick or die or move away. After you've been coming to the Tumbleweed for a while, you can start to pick out the newcomers who'll be back, the ones who'll stay away. They still talk about the time a few years back when the crew from Hollywood toted the bones of Jeremiah Johnson to some grave on the outskirts of town and they all came to the Tumbleweed two nights in a row, then never again, which was almost unheard of. It's an average saloon with a bartender who remembers Buffalo Bill and a painted lady on the wall and mirrors and mahogany. It's perfectly ordinary except that people keep coming back for some reason and they hardly know each other's names.

There are not many women who come to the Tumbleweed, still less who come alone. But somehow I've made my way in, elbowed my way up to the bar, convinced them that I am a spy or a streetwalker. Somehow different from these cowpokes and shopkeepers who get a little lonely during nights in Cody and will sit and reminisce about the olden days. When Wyoming was still a territory. Before the streets were paved. When the tumbleweed blew freely through the streets, rolling as if through a ghost town.

During the days I work at the Buffalo Bill Museum. In the souvenir shop, there's a woman from Staten Island who sells turquoise rings. She claims that just about 'everyone' is moving west. I wish I knew where they are. In the museum I study artifacts and legends of the tribes who lived in the area. At night I go to the Tumbleweed because there isn't anything else to do. It was almost a month before I really noticed him. He was so hidden and dark, so slouched over in that corner of the bar, always the same corner. Never looking up if anyone came in through the barroom doors. He was part of the fixtures, one of the mirrors or stools who never moved and never seemed to come or go. He was your almost classical Indian. The kind you'd never mistake for a Hawaiian or an Eskimo. He had pitch-black straight hair that fell over his brow and around his neck and a squared jaw with high, sharp cheek bones. One trait betrayed his blood line. The bright green eyes that appeared as if they belonged to cats but could possibly be traced back to some American cavalry lieutenant or some fur trader or maybe just one of the cowboys who had passed that way. He was different from the other Indians. The ones who came in already drunk late in the evening and did fake rain dances and begged for money. He was motionless and still and after a time it became clear to me that he was crazy.

O'Grady's in Boston was a different kind of place, but then one would expect the Irish to be different from cowboys and Indians. They have only one natural enemy, the Irish, and that's the English Protestants and a few other groups they can't tolerate like the Jews who were Christ-killers, they said at O'Grady's. But no English Protestant in his right mind would walk into O'Grady's and announce his affiliations. In every bar there's a crazy. At O'Grady's, it was Mr. Murphy who was about eighty-five and did a jig on the tables which he had been performing, according to the patrons, every night for about forty years. If you bought him a drink, he'd tell the story of his life, sobbing the whole time. How his only boy had died in the war.

Which war we never knew. How his wife had run off with another man. How he should have become Ireland's Picasso. That there were no Irish painters because all the Irish did was blabber all the time and how he would have been a great painter if women had not obsessed him. One night Mr. Murphy failed to show; that was how the bartender knew he had died.

The first time I noticed the Indian, really noticed him, it was his feet that caught my eye. Even though his body remained perfectly still and motionless, his feet were doing about fifty miles an hour, vibrating back and forth, nervous as a student taking an exam. I had been coming to the Tumbleweed for over a month when I noticed them for the first time. I had taken a table in the back, something I rarely did because the men always played cards in the back, but that night the tables up front were full. From the back I had a view of the whole Indian and I could see that his feet seemed to be jumping up and down for no reason. For about an hour I watched the motion of his legs. Then I got up and went home. The next night when I returned, I took a seat again in the back so that I could observe the feet of the otherwise motionless Indian. Indians' feet are quiet, I thought to myself, watching him. Or else they are dancing, but this vibrating made no sense. I must have been watching for a long time when I noticed those feet suddenly pause, plant themselves on the ground, rise and walk over toward my table. I heard a chair pulled back and felt him standing just above me and heard him ask 'What?' as if I had summoned him.

At O'Grady's I only spoke with Mr. Murphy once. He had just finished some intricate step of a Highland fling when 'Danny Boy' came on the juke box. Perry Como was singing and Mr. Murphy made a grab for the nearest table which was ours and slumped down. His eyes filled with tears. Suddenly he grabbed me by the arm. 'Marry early,' he said, 'and have many sons.'

But the Tumbleweed was different from O'Grady's. O'Grady's was more like a club where you could go from time to time to visit your friends, pass the hour on your way somewhere else. But the effect of the Tumbleweed on you was like wind on the prairie. It made drifters of us all, itinerants restless and yet somehow aware that we had no place else to go. Cowboys and Indians all drank together. It was some demilitarized zone, some place of refuge like a church in the midst of this once-fighting town.

It was when he sat down and turned slightly my way that I first saw the scar. I had only seen him in profile before and then not very well but now I saw that someone had carved a thin crescent moon out of the side of his left cheek. The crescent began at the bridge of his nose, arching down toward the jaw-bone. I was repulsed by it and yet intrigued. As I looked closely I saw that the scar was so neatly drawn and perfectly formed that it must have been branded or carefully placed there but that it was certainly not the result of some knife fight or an act of random brutality.

When I asked him his name, he said it was a long story but that I should call him, for the time being, Melt Into Her Weaving. He explained that on his vision quest upon becoming a man, he had starved himself for over a week and denied himself sleep. Then he had set out without food or water into the desert and after three days in the midst of a tremendous rainstorm he had found a place on the desert where for some reason the rain did not fall. When he looked at the far ridge of that place, he saw his mother, who had died in childbirth when he was born, and she was weaving for him a blanket and with each movement of the loom, she melted into that weaving until the blanket was complete and she had completely disappeared. He had taken the blanket home when he woke from the deep sleep he had fallen in and when he returned everyone in his tribe agreed that it was the most beautiful blanket anyone had ever seen and that no tribe had ever made one just like it.

But when I called him Melt Into Her Weaving, he shook his head and said that that was no longer his name and that the story was too long to explain and that he would tell me another time what his name had become. We drank another whiskey in silence and then I said I had to go. I left through the front saloon doors and walked slowly through the streets of Cody. The moon overhead was new and cresting. I paused and glanced up at it for the night was very clear and the stars were all out and the breeze felt cool and refreshing, but as I paused, I had the feeling that I was being watched. I turned but saw no one so I set out quickly, heading back to our cabin because I was suddenly afraid.

The next night I did not return to the Tumbleweed. I stayed in the cabin and read but I was restless all evening and the following night I returned. I looked inside but did not see the Indian seated at the bar. I went inside and found a table and ordered a drink. Moments later, it seemed, he appeared. He took his seat at the bar and had a drink. I nodded hello and he nodded back but he did not approach me and I did not approach him. This continued for a week, greeting one another but not speaking. After a week, I suddenly felt an urge to talk to him about his scar for it had haunted me since I saw it the first time and in my mind the scar had grown in proportions so that I knew or at least believed that it was no ordinary scar. No sooner it seemed had I decided that I wanted to speak to the Indian than he rose from the bar and approached my table. He sat down and ordered us two whiskeys which we both knew I would pay for. What startled me when I first looked at his face again was that the scar had changed. What had been a crescent, a thin slip of a moon, was now growing fuller so that nearly a half-moon was carved into the side of his face. It was impossible that, in the past week since we had not spoken, someone had simply enlarged the scar.

He told me that now he wanted to confide in me the whole truth about his scar since he knew that I wanted to know. He ordered another round of drinks and said that it was better not to be too sober. Then he told me the story of his second vision quest.

Normally, there is only one such quest in a man's life, according to Indian custom, but he had remained dissatisfied, plagued with a feeling of uneasiness and restlessness. If he were really Melt Into Her Weaving and if the vision of his mother had given him his adult identity, then it only seemed right that if he went on a second vision quest, he would see the same

vision, thus affirming who he was. His wife, the chief of the tribe, his father, and fellow tribesmen all pleaded with him that what he wanted to do was foolish and wrong but he would not listen. Without the sanction of the tribe, he began to deny himself food and sleep as he had as a boy. For six days he did not eat or sleep. Then he set out into the desert. He wandered an entire day and a night, denying the impulse of his body to pause at a water hole for a drink or to rest in the shade or to sleep during the blackness of night when he could no longer see where he went. The next day he continued walking, falling once onto a cactus, its spines piercing his hands, under the heat of the sun, never once seeking shade or water or rest. He wandered until darkness settled over the desert and he was alone and exhausted and this time he began to grow frightened and was anxious to be home and was even prepared to relinquish his quest. At that moment it came to him. He glanced up and saw the crescent of the moon. There was not a star in the sky, even though the night was clear, but the moon shone a brilliant silver and he suddenly believed himself to be born of that moon and that the moon was simultaneously his mother and his brother and that it would come and touch him so that he would always be the child of darkness, marked and isolated from his race.

He must have fallen asleep, he said, because when he rose it was dawn and the desert was very cool but he felt a burning sensation on his cheek. He touched his face and felt the flesh ooze. He rushed to find a water hole and when he did, he gazed into the water and saw his reflection and saw the shape of a moon, emblazoned on his cheek. When he returned home his wife refused to sleep with him and his children ran away when he called them and his father would never speak to him again. The tribe would not allow him in their midst. Everyone found him ugly and mad and marked by death. 'It is like holding up a mirror every time I move. I see myself reflected everywhere in the sun, in the moon, in this whiskey glass, in the night, in the trees, in your eyes. All I see is myself and my solitude and the moment of my death because when at last this moon wanes on my cheek, as it must one of these days, when it has grown full and then disappears, then I know I will die, though I can't predict it because its flux does not correspond to that of the other moon but one day they will correspond and then I know I will die.'

He grew silent and finished his drink. I did not dare look at his face again for fear that the scar had changed once more. I could only glance at his eyes and see the loneliness branded there which seemed to mimic the scar. I finished my drink as well and he said he would walk me back to my cabin. I agreed and we left the saloon. Outside the night was clear again and I saw the stars but I did not see the moon though I did not look very long or hard. At the door of my cabin, he kissed me passionately on the cheek and pressed me to him and I did not push him away.

I was going to ask him inside but he turned and walked away, even though I called once for him to come back. The night was quiet and I went to bed. From somewhere in the hills around Cody a coyote howled. I tossed and turned for hours, it seemed, never quite drifting to sleep the entire night because each time I came close to sleep the coyote would howl once more so I just lay there and thought of the Indian and of the impression of his lips on my cheek where he had kissed me. The next night I went to the Tumbleweed as usual but he was not there; nor did he come the following night, or the night after that. When I saw that he was not at his usual seat by the bar, I took to walking down the main road, the one that stretches through the center of town, past the line of motels with their signs flashing through the night, down past the museum where the road forks on the way to Yellowstone. The nights when I walked out, it was usually cool and the breeze came down from the mountains, from the passes that were still closed with snow.

The fourth night he was sitting at the bar but when I sat down at my table, he made no sign of recognition, as if he had never seen me before. For some reason, perhaps only habit, I did not approach him or try to speak to him but waited for him to come to my table. He did not and he left before I did. Then for an entire week I did not see him. Each night I went past the

Tumbleweed, looked in, and then began my walk down the main stretch, glancing into the windows of the souvenir shops, contemplating a silver ring, a turquoise medallion I would like to own, following the stretch until I reached the fork in the road. Then I turned back, still gazing into the windows of the stores which helped take my mind off Cody and the night. On my way back at the end of the week one night I ran into one of the regulars leaving the saloon and I asked him if he'd seen him and he said he had that very afternoon in fact. He'd seen him down by the northern road, the one they call the place where the great white giant lives. I was going to get something to eat because I had not eaten all day but then I decided against it; I would overtake him. So I set out that way because I thought I could make it on foot and that it could not be more than three or four miles away. I began down the road, the main road through the center of town that forks off down toward Yellowstone and up toward Red Lodge, the town I first came to when I moved west. I walked down until I came to the fork and turned near the museum, heading north, away from Yellowstone, where the breeze immediately turned cold and I had to button my sweater against the chill.

At the turn-off, I knew he had a good start on me. Unless he were waiting somewhere up on the Red Lodge road, I would never catch him on foot. I didn't bother asking myself what I was doing, going to look for him in the first place. There was a ranch just up the road and the farmer knew me. I passed his place every day on my way to the museum and he called me the lady dude. He'd wave at me from his corral and say 'Mornin', lady dude.' They didn't get many women from the east in Cody. The farmer was working on his tractor under a naked bulb in the barn and I told him what I wanted. He scratched his head. 'I'll bring her back in the morning,' I promised. 'But I have to go up the road and I'll need her.'

He gave me the black mare and was surprised when I showed him I could ride. I galloped around the corral and he nodded. He saw I wouldn't hurt her mouth and I told him I wouldn't fall. I didn't know for certain he'd taken the Red Lodge road but I was fairly certain he wouldn't go into Yellowstone. The rangers knew him and they made him go away because he bothered the tourists. The moon was out and it lit the road and the horse followed easily along. When there was a soft shoulder, I gave her her head and we galloped along; her hooves were silent on the shoulder. I didn't ask myself what I was doing. But I wondered how I'd be without sleep or without food. I come from cities, places that have newspapers and subways. I keep a schedule like everyone else, except I knew the Indian had none and if I didn't hurry, he'd go off into the hills where the snow still blocked the pass and I wouldn't be able to follow him. I knew it didn't matter to him if he slept or not.

He was walking slowly along the road and when I pulled up the mare, he looked up at me. In the dim light I saw his face. He seemed younger than he had and, though he said nothing, I knew he was expecting me. I knew then that what I wanted was for him to give me my name and I knew I didn't have to say it. He hopped up on the back of the mare and pressed his thighs against mine, his bare chest to my back. He was sweating a filmy sweat that seemed to join us together. He reached his hands across my arms and put them on the reins. I let go of the reins and put my hands on the mare's mane. We climbed the road for a while and then he turned off. There wasn't a trail, just an opening in the woods, and we went into the opening. All the time I was aware of his body against my back, his thighs against my thighs and, as if she were aware of it too, the mare followed his slightest move. We walked up into the dark hills until we came to a stone hut which seemed to appear out of nowhere. He slid from the horse and reached out his arms to help me off. I slipped into his arms and for a moment he held me there.

We went into the hut together and he spread two woven blankets on the floor, motioning for me to sit down on the one with the bull on it. His had a huge bird. In the darkness I watched as he sat across from me. This is crazy, I thought, what am I doing here. In his limbs as he rode behind me I had had a memory of something which now came to me. Men are stronger than women in their bodies and being with them is always an act of trust. I felt he could have crushed me if he'd wanted to. Back in Boston I once thought a man who was angry at me was going to throw me out the window. He could have if he'd wanted to. I was almost afraid now but something put me at ease. He was very calm and I sat cross-legged in front of him, the way he was sitting.

In the morning when I woke, he was still sitting in the same position. I had curled up and gone to sleep though I didn't remember when. Though I'd slept, I still hadn't eaten. 'I must get the horse back,' I said; 'I promised.' He nodded. We rose, rolled up the blankets and got back on the mare, but we were riding further into the hills, not toward the ranch or the museum where I had to be at work by nine. 'I have to turn back,' I said, but he kept going further into the hill and so I didn't say anything more.

I'm not sure for how long we rode but we rode until we reached a butte. We had to lead the mare up by hand because it was too steep for us to be on her. She resisted because there was no grass on the butte. I was tired and hungry. My legs ached and I wanted to bathe. On the butte he rolled out the blankets again and this time he unbuttoned my shirt and made me take it off. Then he made me take off my pants. He only had his pants on. I lay down on the blanket and he ran his hands across my legs, up my belly. He pressed his face to my ear, he rubbed his face into my hair.

It was dusk when I opened my eyes again and realized I was a horse thief. 'I've got to get the mare back,' I said. 'They think I've stolen her.' He nodded and pulled me back to him. I looked at his scar which I had hardly noticed since I met him on the road. It was just a thin sliver, almost nonexistent. I was aware of the numbness in my belly. I hadn't eaten in two days. He agreed that they'd be looking for me soon, so I'd have to either go further north with him or else stay there on the butte a day or so more. I told him I was too hungry to decide and I spent the night curled into a ball while he sat staring beside me. At dawn we climbed back on the mare and rode. We rode down the butte and across the valley. We rode that entire day and most of the next. I knew we couldn't be far from Red Lodge and at times I saw the hint of distant towns, cabin lights flickering on the hill, but we stayed clear of the lights. Each night he rolled out the blankets. We lay on one and he covered us with the other. In the night his breath warmed my neck.

One day it turned very hot but we rode all day in the sun. My lips were cracking and my throat was very parched; the numbness seemed to grow inside my belly, seemed to creep into my limbs, and as we rode and his body pressed against mine, I felt myself grow weaker and weaker. I had no more resistance to anything. The mare stopped for water or to graze but we didn't and I knew we wouldn't. The day it was very hot I almost fainted. I started slipping from the saddle and I felt him catching me. A rattlesnake startled the mare and she reared. With his knife the Indian cut the snake in two. He stripped it of its skin and threw the flesh away, though I thought he might save it to cook but he didn't and we went another day without food. That night I didn't feel well. The cool of the desert crept into my bones. He covered me with both blankets and watched over me. I fell asleep thinking I was dying and that I had to do something to save myself. I felt as if the water had left my body.

In the night I dreamed of a lavender horse. It was the same color as a sweater I had back in my cabin, the one I wished I had with me to protect me from the cold. It was a beautiful lavender horse, the color of tiny flowers, and I was privileged to ride. I got on the horse and started to ride. Crowds seemed to be watching me. They watched as I rode to the edge of a butte and suddenly the lavender horse began to fall. It fell and fell, over and over, twisting upon itself, its legs tied into knots, leaving me behind, and everyone watched in horror. As it fell, it grew darker and darker, moving into deep shades of purple, until it reached the bottom of the butte where it kicked its legs up into the air, fell over onto its back, and died. And as it died it turned black, turned into a regular black horse. I woke with a start and the Indian stood above me, holding the mare by the reins, and I knew he was going to leave. 'Tell me, what did you

see?' he said. And I told him about the lavender horse. He said
it was the horse for special journeys only made by a privileged
few and that such journeys are not special if they go on forever,
but they must end. With his fingertips, he tapped the place
where his heart was inside his chest; 'I will always take you
with me,' he said, 'and you will always be with me,' and my
name to him would be Lavender Horse because I'd given him
the special journey. He said you never really know anything
until you know its name.

I wanted to follow but he refused. It was too dangerous and
he wasn't very popular in these parts. He said we each had to
go back to our people and I should make up any story about
where I'd been but I shouldn't tell them the truth. He'd look for
me in the spring.

He took the horse because he needed her. He said they'd
believe me if I told them she was stolen. I've never stolen anything in my life. I argued with him but he promised it would be
all right. I looked and saw the scar the size of a half moon and
remembered that the night before the moon had almost reached
its half. He bent down and kissed me again. It was just daybreak
and the morning light glistened on the mare, a heavy purplish
light, the kind in the sky just before sunrise, I watched him ride
her away until I couldn't see them any more.

The numbness inside me turned to real hunger. I was starving.
I hadn't noticed it before. My body was feeding upon itself. I
searched the ground for food but there wasn't so much as a root
to be eaten so I set out toward the paved road. On the road, I
got a hitch with a trucker hauling soda pop and he gave me a
Fanta orange which I gulped down. He saw something had
happened to me. 'You OK, miss? You don't look so good.' I told
him I'd been kidnapped and asked him to drop me off at the
fork on the Red Lodge road. The farmer was prepared to have
me arrested until he saw the shape I was in. He told me my
face was red and the skin cracked and my eyes swollen and red.
I told him about the kidnapping and gave him fifty dollars for
the mare. He gave me some cornbread and a slab of bacon to
eat which made me sleepy. I told him I'd rest, then I'd report

the incident to the proper authorities. He didn't seem to care about the horse now that he had the money and I never reported anything, not even for appearance's sake, because I knew I could never tell anyone where I'd been and that if I started to lie I'd get caught in a tangle of lies.

The snow started up north; I knew I wouldn't see him before spring and by then I'd be gone. I wanted to look for him again but I remembered what happened when he went looking for his mother a second time. Sometimes at night as the weather was turning, I'd wake and feel someone had covered me as I slept. I'd go outside for a breath of air. The moon burned my cheek like sunlight. I'm sure people were talking about me but there wasn't much I could do.

The Salesman

IN THE TOWN where I grew up in the late 1920s, when we were very poor, there was a legend that was common knowledge to all. It was said that across the river, deep into the foreign lands of Ohio, beyond the Cuyahoga burial grounds, past ravines and scattered swamps, there was a hill. The hill was protected by a brambled path, iron gates, and a labyrinth of overgrown hedges. It was camouflaged by bougainvillea imported from Jamaica which had long ago grown wild and extended itself like spider webs over all the plants and trees so that in spring the hill was a vast blanket of bougainvillea, its branches reaching into the sea of brambles and patches of wild strawberries. In that southern tip of the state, the rains came early and in summer the climate can be almost tropical as yellow swallowtails and tiger monarchs flit from vine to vine.

When spring came, men - sailors, businessmen, vagabonds - all tried to make their way through the maze of lianas and climbing vines, clamber up the serried thickets, past the iron gates, and not succumb to the sweet scent of bougainvillea. If they were successful, they reached a moat which at one time was said to have housed real crocodiles during the warmer months, though this seems doubtful, but which then contained only a few leeches and stagnant water with a pale green slime floating on the top. And if they reached the moat, if they crossed the tiny footbridge, they arrived at the castle of the Duchess of

Zoe from whose great doors they were immediately escorted away.

That was not the legend. That was the fact. Though it was a bad time for us and I'd never seen a castle, I knew it existed. Even the postmaster said so. The legend was about the traveling salesman of musical instruments. He was employed by a musical instrument manufacturing concern in the East and he went from door to door, visiting the rural churches, the remote schoolhouses, the spinster music teachers in their rundown cabins, peddling his wares and performing as a one-man jazz band.

From time to time, it was said, he went to the castle. He would stand at the footbridge, playing on his harmonica or his saxophone, while his elusive notes permeated the garden and penetrated the balcony windows and her solitude. The legend was that he enticed the duchess from her inner chambers where she emerged from the self-imposed isolation in which she had lived since her husband and two children were lost in the First World War. Since their deaths, she had not had a sane or lucid moment. She brought her fortunes to America and searched for the most obscure and insignificant spot on the map and there she constructed her fortress and lived, hidden from all men and women, except for her chambermaid and the keeper of her rose garden. She was said to be so beautiful that all the mirrors within a three-mile radius reflected only her image, but this we could hardly believe.

She saw no one and no one ever saw her until she stepped onto her balcony that night and invited the salesman in. She asked him to play all his instruments for her and this he did. He played the flute and the clarinet, the tambourine and the violin, all the instruments contained within his sample case. He devised an instrument from a washtub and a rubber band and this he played for her as well. She had a harpsichord in the main ballroom to which no one had ever danced and he played it for her after tuning it. She invited him to dinner but he refused. He had a wife and small children and had to continue along his route. She bought one of each of his instruments, which was more money than he usually saw on his entire route, and he knew he was obliged to her. She led him into a dining room of crystal chandeliers and velvet curtains. They dined at a long table where he felt very foolish. After dinner, he roamed marble corridors, his saxophone resounding endlessly through the desolate halls. He stayed that night. And the next. And when he left four days later, no matter where he went or what he did, he could not get her out of his mind for the rest of his life. He was my father.

I knew him well, as well as I could. He came down to the dock where I kept my launch, the one I hired out for fishing. Once a month he paid me a quarter to take him across the river and another quarter to fetch him three weeks later when he appeared, always at the same time on the right day, on the opposite side. Ohio to me was a vast, uninhabitable land, wild and mean, but he was not afraid. Once he had almost toured Europe as a violinist but then the Depression came and he turned to this line of work. It wasn't a bad living. The rural schools and churches all had bands and he could repair and tune anything that made a sound. He'd hum as I rowed, usually old river songs, songs he'd picked up on steamers in his many journeys, and he'd teach me these, if the river wasn't frozen and I could row him. If it was frozen, which wasn't often, he'd hike up to the bridge, but either way he could hike off to the Hiawatha Trail once across and go on to where he was going. I think he liked me best because I never asked any questions, never pestered him about where he went or if it was true what they said about him. I never asked the way my mother and brothers and other relatives used to ask but there was something in the wind, I could tell, because as we got closer to the river bank not far from where she lived, the breeze seemed to shift and the trees rustled and the air sweetened as if it was lilac time.

This went on for years, with me rowing him across and him handing me a quarter and then me meeting him three weeks later and getting another quarter, and we always had this understanding because I never asked where he'd been and he let me grow up the way I wanted. It went on until one day when we reached the other side he asked me to please moor my boat and come with him. He was getting older and he said he needed an assistant now. I argued that I couldn't leave my little boat. What else did I have? Who would row it back? And probably it would be gone when I returned. Then how would we get back? He laughed and said I was just being silly and assured me it would be there when we returned and that he wanted me, only me, to come with him. I told him to ask one of the boys, for I had many brothers and they were always ready to pack up and go anywhere, but he said it had to be me, because I had rowed him all these years. In the end I saw that I had to go and could not refuse because no one else understood him as I did.

We tied the boat to a tree and covered it with leaves. Then he started down the path into the woods and I followed quickly behind. I was surprised he could walk that fast but he kept up the pace for miles it seemed, moving deeper and deeper into those woods with me following as best as I could. We walked until we came to the hill with the brambled path and the wild bougainvillea and we began to climb. We reached the gates and my father quickly unlatched them. They were beautiful gates with bronze animals along their crest. Then we climbed higher until we came to what was really a large villa. There was no moat, no drawbridge, no sentinels standing guard. But there was an endless garden of roses, mostly the red ones called matadors, and blue butterflies fluttered past. We had to wait until dusk, my father said, because that was the best time. So we waited, he sitting silently next to me, humming the way he did the old river songs. But I knew what he liked was that I didn't ask questions and so I said nothing, waiting for dusk. When the sky darkened and the moon appeared over the top of the hill, my father pointed to a stone bench at the side of the balcony and he told me to sit there. He took his harmonica from one of his two suitcases and began to play a quiet melody. It was soft and sad like the call of the mourning dove, a melody from the South. He played and a chill came into the air and soon I saw a shadow come toward the balcony, but the curtain was in the way and I knew that my father had had me sit on the stone bench because I would only be able to see a silhouette, and that not very well. I saw a vague profile, not her face, but I saw my father's. A tired, haggard man with many burdens, the lines on his brow seemed to disappear, his eyes brightened and he wore a peculiar look of contentment. It was as if he'd seen some rare and perfect bird and, even though I was still young, I knew that he and the duchess may have eaten at the same table or slept in the same house but they never touched and never would and it even seemed possible at that moment that they'd never even spoken.

We didn't talk much about it as we rowed back but we both accepted that a new routine had settled in. Now I rowed him across, walked the long walk through the woods behind him, went with him to the castle which now I knew wasn't a castle at all but a villa. Then he went on along his route and I reached home by dawn with my mother always fussing about where I'd been. But I kept our secret and even though she'd ask every day, three weeks later when I fetched him on the opposite bank, I hadn't said a word. In this I was my father's daughter. Then he'd rest a week and his eternal pilgrimage would begin again, the restless life of the salesman. He and my mother seemed to ignore one another and for one week in four he'd sleep in her bed and eat her food without either of them acting as if the other were there. Then, weary, getting older, my father would set out again and I went with him. Once as I rowed him across and he seemed distracted, I gathered my nerve. 'Did you sleep with her?' I asked. 'The way the rumors said you did?' But his eyes just gave me a strange, quizzical stare as if he didn't know what language I was speaking. Sometimes on the long walk, he'd give me a flute or a clarinet, not to help him carry but to learn how to play, and it wasn't more than a few years before I could play almost as well as he.

I watched him grow older. His legs seemed to shorten and grow squat and his belly swelled. His hair turned a moonlight silver and he couldn't see so well any more. Crow's feet formed at the corners of his eyes. He used a walking stick now and I carried one of the suitcases. Soon I was carrying both of them. He needed help more and more and sometimes he stumbled on the path he knew like the back of his hand. I stood back and watched, mostly helpless to do anything because he was always a stubborn man. I watched as he grew weaker and weaker until one day he told me that we wouldn't be going to see the duchess any more. This time I was filled with questions, I could not contain them. Had they quarreled? Was she sick? Was he? Was the trip too much for him? Perhaps if we drove. But he shook his head at everything I said. It had nothing to do with any of that. It was just that he'd decided to shorten his route. If he reversed his direction and skipped going to see her, he'd save over a week. He could do the entire route in two weeks and have two weeks to rest. It would be much easier. He knew what he needed so there wasn't any sense arguing with him. He said I should go, just one more time, and stand under the balcony and play something I'd learned from him and that way she'd know he wasn't going to be coming back.

I couldn't see the harm. I knew he was getting older and I wouldn't want him to be disappointed over this simple request. I wouldn't want him to die with me wishing I had done just this one last thing. So that day as we reached the other side, he was smiling and seemed very content. He helped me moor the boat. Then he followed the trail along the river bank while I took the path through the woods. I walked on the path which seemed overgrown to me but perhaps it was just because I was lonely. I walked the road I knew by heart, deeper and deeper, until I came to the hill. I knew the routine. I climbed the hill, played the harmonica at the footbridge, then went and sat in the garden near the balcony until dusk. The air was turning chilly when I rose from the wooden bench and began to play on the flute. I played one of the old river songs until I saw her shadow, strange, unreal. It seemed to loom up against the walls. Even before I saw her, before she reached the balcony, I knew I'd made a mistake. I knew I never should have moored my boat the first time. Ohio is a wild, dangerous place. And now I knew my boat would be gone or else have a hole dug out of it when I returned. I cursed myself for coming here, but I knew he didn't do it on purpose. I knew he hadn't meant to lead me astray by shortening his journey, though he had infinitely lengthened mine. What else was there for him to do? He was getting so old, even as he'd played for her in the past few months, his face had not lit up but remained old, filled with its burdens. He had not seemed rejuvenated as we left but more tired than before. I knew he wouldn't lead me this way unless it had to be done, because he was my father and he always did the right thing.

I knew even before she stood on the balcony, even before I saw her – and she was so beautiful – that she never changed but just went on and on, year after year, looking the way she always looked. That was part of her madness. And I knew that she didn't mind that I'd come. She'd been expecting me for some time. As she looked down and smiled at me, I thought how all I'd ever wanted was to just take him back and forth across the river. But this, I'd never wanted this. I never thought it would lead to this. I'd tell him so. I'd tell him if I ever got the chance, if he hadn't gone for good along the path on the river bank, along a southern route he'd never taken before.

Holland

꧁ ꧂

MY GREAT-AUNT EVA had patience as if she could wait for
eternity; that was why when she died, mean and ugly
and absorbed by her pain, and we buried her in the family plot
in an August heat wave, everyone was surprised. No one ever
expected her to die, or to change in any way. With both of our
parents working when we were children, my four brothers and
I spent most of our days growing up at great-aunt Eva's. She
was a spinster and looking back, I feel certain, a virgin. Indeed,
she seemed a fortress of virginity, but, perhaps because she was
proud, taciturn, and ultimately strange, an archive of family
rumors surrounded her.

According to legend, she had fallen in love with a man named
Jake when she was eighteen. He lived on the outskirts of town,
near the rural districts, and Eva and her family lived to the
north, some miles away in the heart of the city. Every Sunday
Jake rode from the south where the rural districts began to pick
up Eva in his buggie. Eva dressed in her finest taffeta with a
muff and a veil regardless of the weather and, at one o'clock
sharp, his buggie arrived out front. He never phoned because
they had no phone, and he never wrote. He never came inside,
except once, the first time he picked her up. It was simply the
arrangement as everyone understood it and it continued for
nine years, almost driving Eva's father into the grave. One
Sunday Jake didn't arrive. Eva went into her room and shut the

door. Every Sunday thereafter until just before she died, she'd go into her room and shut the door for the entire afternoon, emerging just when the sun began to go down, because that was the hour when Jake's carriage had always brought her home. Occasionally, she called my grandmother into the room and asked my grandmother how she looked. Because Eva was dressed each Sunday in her muff and veil, prepared to depart. When I was born and growing up mostly at Eva's house, I never once went there on a Sunday because that was her day with Jake.

My mother worked in a bakery, making sweet-smelling breads, and my father worked at the city dump. Their work was as diametrically opposed as their personalities were; they weren't unhappy, just opposed. So the first seven years of my life and my brothers' were spent at Eva's because when our parents weren't working, they were fighting, and because no one else in the family volunteered for the job.

Perhaps because of her years waiting for Jake, Eva was very patient with us, even though she would never have children of her own. If we fought among ourselves or cried over some minor injustice, she had a sure-fire remedy which she employed only in extreme cases. 'You are not behaving,' she'd say, 'so it will have to be the supreme punishment for bad children.'

Great-aunt Eva led us into the back room. Her dressing table had piles of ivory and tortoise-shell combs, ivory-set nail buffers and black silk fans, and the hat pins she'd collected stuck into a tomato-shaped pin cushion. There was always the faint odor of a woman about the place which came from the dozens of small colored bottles containing hair oils and stale perfumes. There was also the scent of cedar because all the hats and boas and skirts were kept in the cedar closet. And there was the brass elephant with the chipped tusks, though he disappeared just before she died and was not found until years later, buried in the garden, where we assumed Eva had buried him. In the top drawer of the dresser were perhaps a dozen hand mirrors with petitpoint embroidery on their backs, and on the side of the dresser was a magazine rack which contained copies of *Vogue* from the 1920s. Though we knew all of these objects in Eva's dressing room by heart, none of them was the supreme punishment. She pointed at the various objects until we had to plead with her to get it down from where it was hidden on the uppermost shelves behind the hats.

She stood on the step ladder, fumbled for a while, talking to herself, until she produced a small glass object that fit into the palm of her hand. Inside a boy and a girl were on a seesaw, their backs turned to us so that we never saw their faces. Both wore wooden shoes and were in front of a gingerbread house. The girl wore a blue jumper and a hat and had long braids and the boy wore puffy trousers, a red vest, and a blue sailor's cap. Eva shook the paperweight so that a snowstorm began, even in the middle of summer, and blue and white flakes fell slowly, making the seesaw go up and down, and we stopped fighting and started betting on whether the boy or the girl would be higher when the blizzard ceased. Then Eva pointed to the word inscribed beneath that self-contained snowstorm, and, even though most of us could not yet read, we all knew what was written and we said the word in unison as if recognizing it for the first time: it read 'Holland.'

Years later, I remembered my first love. Most of us, it seems, fall in love for the first time not in response to the totality of an individual, because this requires too much thought and we might never manage to fall in love, but rather in response to some detail about his or her person. It's the love of this detail which permits us to love with abandon. For a woman, it might be the flex of the biceps, the sincerity of a smile, the promise of a Harvard degree. I was immune to all of these, due perhaps to an abundance of brothers. Instead, I fell hopelessly, and, as my brother Brice would add, pathetically, in love at the age of seventeen with a totally inappropriate object for my affections, an overgrown Swede named Holland Bjorstrom.

He was built like a sequoia, and towered over me, hardly fitting straight-on through a doorway. His eyes were the color of maple syrup and I never saw him crack a smile or say an

intelligent word in the three years I loved him. So it must have been the name. My brothers could not tolerate him. Because he hulked so large, he seemed unusually ugly, but they did not hold that against him. Brice would have nothing to do with him because he was prematurely bald and Brice had been born with a fear of aging. Stephen, my second brother, wanted nothing to do with him because he insisted on playing tennis and could never so much as tap the ball without having it sail over the fence. Joshua, my third brother, was indifferent to anyone who couldn't play chess, and James, the baby, was intrigued with Holland as one might be with a brontosaurus.

I had a slightly different problem with Holland. He was an umbrella salesman. Actually he helped manage his family's rainwear factory and would someday take over the company and become a very wealthy man. It was not easy to find topics of interest to discuss with an umbrella salesman. We talked about rain as much as we could. Holland had as many different terms for rain as Bedouins for camel dung. There were light drizzles, soft drizzles, spring drizzles, threatening drizzles, normal drizzles, and dry drizzles, which I never managed to identify. There were downpours and deluges, drenchings and hurricanes, precipitations and evaporations, fogs and smogs and mists (which came close to dry drizzles) and dews, thunderstorms, lightning storms, electrical storms, Nor'easters, sleet and hail, April showers and flash floods, light rains, heavy rains, monsoons, and then, though he said it was very rare, just plain rain. If Holland ever revealed to me a glimmer of his experiencing pleasure, it was when it rained. What others bemoaned, he applauded. What ruined the best planned picnics and the most awaited softball games, he rejoiced in. Rain to Holland was money in the bank; he prayed for floating currency, for liquid assets and cash flow.

Eva used to say that she wanted to go to Holland because Holland had been good to the Jews during the Second World War. Eva's father had been Jewish and she considered herself a Jew. She said that in Holland the king had put a Jewish star on his sleeve when Hitler said all the Jews must wear stars. No one except Brice, because he believed in truth above everything else, ever took the trouble of correcting her. He said time after time that it was not a king from Holland, but King Christian of Denmark, and he didn't really wear a star; it was just a rumor.

Eva would hear nothing of this. For her, history's only function was the molding of events to support the idea. We suspected that Holland had something to do with Jake and that it must have been Jake who gave her that paperweight because she was loyal to its word as if to some oath. As the years went by, she grew more and more adamant that it was the Dutch who saved the Jews, that the Dutch had even made a significant contribution to the ending of the World War, that Hans Brinker really skated on silver skates and saved the city by putting a finger in a dike.

One winter she bought us skates which she spray-painted silver in the garage; we were supposed to skate along the Wisconsin border a mile from where we were living. On u.s. 78 to be specific. A state trooper brought us home and Eva cursed at him from the back room. She took us to the side streets and had us skate there. She took us down to the Fox River in March and we skated but James fell through the ice where it had thawed. That was when Mother decided Eva was getting too old to handle us any more. So we saw less and less of her and since we were in school, there was no reason to spend much time at her house. As we grew older, eating Dutch chocolate and going dutch on dates became jokes among us. Eva still talked about Amsterdam as if she had lived there all her life, as if tulips blossomed all year right on the canals like lily pods. Once a year, as soon as Brice was old enough to drive, we piled into the car and drove two hundred miles to the tulip festival in Holland, Michigan, and we would bring back as many tulip bulbs and flowers as we could load into the car and afford. That was the only thing we ever really did for Eva.

She planted the bulbs out back and put so many bunches of tulips into water in the house that she had to fill the goldfish bowl which was always stocked with goldfish. Some of them managed to live for several years. The fish swam, darting through the tulip stems like slalom skiers.

Eva never once mentioned the man we all knew she waited for each Sunday. Never uttered his name or offered a word of explanation or ever referred to Sunday or what she did on that day. My grandmother said they'd never known Jake's last name or where they had met or what he did or why he stopped coming to the house. Only once did I hear of Eva confiding her feelings about men, and that was to me. She had heard through Brice that I was heartsick over a breakup between myself and 'some leviathan.'

Eva took me aside one afternoon and told me she had been surprised to learn there had been any such romance going on and was shocked that I'd been behaving in this manner for at least three years. 'Did he touch you?' she asked. I shook my head. I wasn't lying; I am certain that touching never crossed Holland's mind. 'That's good.' A smile broke across her features, spreading to maniacal proportions, 'Because if a man touches a woman's body, her whole body disintegrates.' The dark circles beneath her eyes seemed to darken even more, her hand trembled as she placed it on my shoulder. 'Her body crumbles to nothing. To waste. Even in marriage, there is no escape.' I had been warned against premarital relations but never with the threat of disintegration and never had I been warned against a husband's touch. She grabbed me as firmly as she could on both shoulders. 'Promise me,' she said, 'promise me, that a man will never touch you.' I looked into her eyes. They were filled with rage; and so I promised, the way a politician will promise something he would like to keep but knows is impossible and so he hopes that, in the face of future promises kept, this first one will be forgotten or at least forgiven.

Though Eva did not speak of Jake, she did speak about the man whom she claimed had been the inspiration for the purchase of the paperweight. It was the story she gave and, whether it was true or not, we came to understand that she believed it was true. When she was a very young girl, she said, she had been introduced to John Holland, a Dutchman, the famous inventor and designer of submarines. She said she'd been introduced to him before nature had made her a woman and that he had immediately asked our great-grandfather for her hand when she came of age. Brice, who eventually became a newspaperman, the profession which seemed to suit best his thirst for truth and seemingly paradoxical love for the sensational, checked the facts. John Holland had been an Irishman, not a Dutchman. He had been happily married for years and had one foot in the grave when Eva claimed he made his proposal.

Eva was never quite able to explain to anyone's satisfaction how it was that she had come to meet the inventor of submarines (or to verify that it was she who had turned him down because she was then in love with a young British soldier). Eva said she met him in the house in Kensington where she had lived for a year with her father and her younger brothers and sisters while the family was in the process of emigrating to America. Her father, an engineer, knew many interesting people in London and John Holland had been one of them. One day he had glimpsed her in the parlor and the next day he came calling. He walked up the steps in a black morning coat and top hat with an umbrella tucked under his arm, even though there was no sign of rain, and asked if Miss Eva were at home. That was how they had known he was a gentleman.

I met my husband on a ski slope in Vermont. Actually I did not meet him on the slope. I was skiing down the mountain and he was going up on a rope tow. He observed me skiing off the trail and into the woods, disappearing behind a grove of trees. A blizzard had begun and it was almost an hour's time down the mountain so he did not feel it would be forward of him to help. He left the rope tow and skied over. He found me with my skis locked and crossed at the ankles, my bindings not released, unable to turn over. He picked me up, straightened my skis, and brushed the snow from my legs. He led me out of the woods, back onto the trail. By now the blizzard seemed in earnest. Enormous flakes of blue-white snow fell around us and we were unable to see more than a few feet in front of us. He suggested we complete the run together. I told him I had been out over an hour and a half and that now my feet were numb.

We wended our way slowly along a narrow path. I followed his bright red parka and blue cap as he turned and dipped. When we reached the lodge, he removed my boots because my hands were too numb. He packed my toes, which were very white, in snow that he collected from outside. He put my hands in ice water that he took from the cafeteria. The pain of the blood returning to my limbs was excruciating and he rubbed my neck to help me relax. After a few minutes, he massaged very gently my feet and hands. He brought me hot chocolate and continued working on my fingers and toes until the pain was gone. I never recovered the sensation in two of my toes.

We checked our gear and went into the bar. It was already getting dark and the sun was setting. A stark red crimson crept over the land, turning the snow into mountains of pink. The storm had settled. In the bar we sat by the fire with a view of the mountains, sipping glass after glass of Irish coffee. We were getting drunk. It occurred to us, when it was finally dark outside, that we hadn't exchanged names. I told him mine and he said his was John, but his good friends called him Jack. He spoke it softly so that the sound of the word was almost indistinguishable from the crackling of the fire and I had to lean very far forward in order to hear. It was Jack, not Jake, but that was close enough for me and I made a mental note that I would not go out with him for more than six months unless he seemed honest in his intentions and that somehow I'd expiate the life-long sufferings of my great-aunt Eva.

When I took Jack home to the Midwest to meet my family, great-aunt Eva shut herself in her room and refused to see us. Though the rest of the family gave us a warm reception, Eva wouldn't leave her room.

I pounded on the door and told her that I had loved her more than anyone else had loved her and more than I had loved anyone when I was a child. I told her I was moving East and

she would not see me for some time. I told her Jack was upset
by her behavior, which he was, and that everyone would soon
be fighting on her account. My pleas went unheeded. Patience,
it seems, has another side, and Eva's, when it turned sour,
became an impenetrable stubbornness, a wall which she now
effectively constructed between herself and the world. This
childless, husbandless woman who, without bitterness, had
reared five children without laying a hand on them, whose most
extreme punishment was the soporific effect of a snowstorm in
a paperweight, had closed the door on me. The night before our
wedding, I pounded once more on the door, exhausted and
drained from my efforts. It was then that I heard what sounded
like a scratching, a tiny rasping noise coming from behind me.
I pressed my ear to the door but all I was able to make out were
the words 'a promise is a promise,' and those were Eva's last
spoken words to me.

On the day of our wedding, she stayed in her room, Brice told
me, until we were several hundred miles away; and then when
she finally did leave her room, she was dressed in deep mourning, a long black dress, black veil, and gloves, and she wore that
costume until the day she died. They were never certain for
what or for whom she was mourning. But if my name were
spoken, she whispered 'harlot' or 'strumpet' or 'hussy' under
her breath, just loud enough so that Joshua would hear and
that would drive him from the house in a rage and she would
sit, laughing to herself.

Once, perhaps in a moment of weakness, she clasped Stephen's hand, lifted her veil, and sighed, saying that she had
received a telegram and that the man who used to come calling
on her had died. For once, apparently, Brice didn't bother re-
futing the fact that no telegram had arrived. Whether Jake had
died or not, and perhaps somehow she did know, she never
locked herself in her room again on a Sunday, but sat gazing
out the window in the parlor. Whether or not the Dutch saved
the Jews or she had met a man named John Holland or received
a telegram, one thing was certain. Eva was dying.

Her hair turned silver in a matter of weeks. Her face, which
had been smooth and sculpted, assumed a permanent, wrinkled

frown. She grew strange. All books, papers, and pencils had to be placed at right angles. The television was kept on at all times but no sound was allowed. If someone wanted to hear the news, they had to wait until Eva was sound asleep. She shut the cat in the fruit cellar until he nearly died of starvation and James finally found him, a shadow of his former self. She yelled if anyone left a fingerprint on a table or made a lampshade or painting crooked, but while she shrieked at fingerprints, she would not permit dusting. She refused to open the mail. She screamed at all solicitors and cancelled her milk deliveries. And, in a final act of defiance, she killed off all her goldfish one by one, those fish that had swum between tulip stems, by spearing them with her antique hatpins that she kept in the tomato-shaped pin cushion.

She refused to eat anything that was not chocolate or had chocolate in it and they had to invent the most disgusting concoctions in order to persuade her to eat something that resembled a balanced meal. She gave up sleeping and developed bistre circles like half-moons beneath her eyes, and she would doze off at dinner or in the middle of a sentence when she could not keep her eyes open any longer, but in five or ten minutes she would waken with a start and curse herself for letting go. Late at night, when the rest of the town was sound asleep, Brice would see the light shining beneath her door and he knew that inside Eva was sitting up, reading the book she had requested from the library - a pictorial history of submarines.

Almost two years later, long after I had relinquished any hope of hearing from Eva again, assured by my husband that she was mad or senile or both, I received a letter. I was pregnant with my first child and surprised to see the shaky scrawl on the envelope, like a child's scribblings. I removed the letter from the envelope. 'If it's a girl,' she had written, 'don't name her Eva.'

One morning, the boys told me, she rose from her sickbed, went to a drawer in the back room, and took out a stash of money which she had hidden away. She put the money into piles and told the boys to whom each of the piles would go; she said that this money had not been designated in her will. I was not mentioned. Then she found a bag of sewing and darned some socks and sewed on some buttons. She dusted and made a list of repairs that would have to be done. She straightened out the dresser and arranged her room so that it was exactly as it had been some sixty years before when Jake came calling. Then she went into the parlor and told the boys that she needed some sleep and they should wake her in an hour.

The funeral was simple and sad but no one cried except for my grandmother and me and a small, shrunken man in a heavy black wool suit who sobbed endlessly into a handkerchief. He stood back near a toppled-over headstone, his face red and puffy from grief. He left just as Eva was lowered into the ground, and tossed a fistful of soil over her before disappearing. Later, it seemed that no one had any idea who he was and my grandmother vehemently denied that he was the man who'd courted Eva so long ago. 'That man was tall and handsome,' my grandmother said. 'Not like this silly old one.'

When the casket was being lowered, James kicked the ground, called Eva an old nut, and walked away. Joshua chewed gum throughout the entire ceremony. Brice and Stephen were off to the tennis courts as soon as the first shovelfuls of dirt were dropped down. My mother complained of the heat and my father rocked back and forth on the balls of his feet. When I returned after a week at home, Jack met me at LaGuardia. He took my bags, kissed me perfunctorily on the cheek and muttered something about it being a waste of good money to do homage to a fool. We drove back on that hot August afternoon in silence, while our daughter slept soundly in the back. Once I put my hand on his knee but I felt him go tense and I took my hand away.

We crossed Manhattan and entered the Holland Tunnel. Traffic was bumper to bumper. Cars backed up behind us for miles it seemed, ahead of us we couldn't tell how far. We leaned back in our seats as we moved slowly, like a battalion, deeper and deeper into the tunnel.

The tunnel was a yellow-gray. Its heat seemed visible, swaying in waves like a snake. Motorists were impatient, honking,

leaning out of their windows. It was difficult to breathe. I
thought of Eva in her small, narrow subterranean cave. I
thought of the light that shone beneath her door those nights
when she would not sleep and spent hours poring over the
history of submarines. Not dreaming of their inventor but
studying those narrow machines, learning every valve, every
hatch.

We had not moved for some time and Jack was slow to tell
me that we were stalled. He said not to panic because all around
us cars were stalled, overheated like us, or just plain tired, and
that we would need a tow. I panic in small places. I always
have. I've told Jack that I want a burial at sea, my body floating
freely among fishes, a snack for spawning bluefish. That I would
sprout gills and reign immortal, but that he should never close
me up in the ground.

'Well, did the old lady leave you anything?' Jack asked, trying
to make conversation. I could not fault his dislike of Eva. He'd
never seen the woman, never spoken to her. He hadn't spent
years listening to the rumors which only her mysterious and
self-imposed silence evoked, rumors which perhaps all had
some truth in them, though none had all the truth which Brice
hungered after, and that truth had died as intact as I believed
Eva's body had been. Surely no man had brought about its
disintegration.

Her final words for me had been to the point. She did not
mention me by name or say what it was she was leaving me,
but no one contested it. The lawyer read, 'And to my great-
niece, the supreme punishment for bad children.' And then he
shrugged his shoulders and asked if anyone could explain to
what or to whom the deceased had referred.

Vanishing Animals

YESTERDAY WE WENT to a buffalo auction. Ernie said it would be a novelty; in fact it was rather banal. Those mangy beasts, their hair matted with sage or worn away by so much rubbing against the dry earth, stood with their legs chained, tugging nervously against the steel links. Their stench, as provocative as their baritone moos, permeated the vast, open plain. It was cruel, I thought, but Ernie said it was interesting. We could bring one home to our West Side apartment and it would be a conversation piece in New York. We'd ride it, he said, in Central Park and people would pass and inquire, 'Is that the latest model Peugot?' or 'Is that the city's new mounted patrol?' and I would reply 'No, it's an American buffalo.'

He has brought me here to cure me, the way some go to Hot Springs or Lourdes, to their faith healers or their local mounte-banks, and others to some highly recommended tarot reader or Mayos or a visiting guru, and a few still turn their hopes to heaven. He has brought me home. Actually these mountains are not mine but his. I come from the low, flat lands where the dullness of the geography is compensated for by the extremes of climate. But for Ernie this place is the cure-all, the answer to whatever ails you, a place to rest your bones a spell. 'Fresh mountain air, long brisk walks, hardly a traffic jam.' And since we are alike in so many ways, he believes that we must share the same panaceas. I need magic, a miracle, I tell him, and ask for a burning bush, some relevant answer in a fortune cookie. He has brought me here to forget about Aaron and last spring because it has been six months already but somehow everything serves as a reminder, everything seems to conspire.

He takes my hand as we wander past the rows of guffawing cowboys who are wearing Stetsons and cowboy boots, with their horses tied to the hitching posts at the side of the big corral. An Indian with blood-shot eyes and crippled, arthritic hands sells me a turquoise ring which he claims to have made with those hands. 'It is a sign of good luck and endless possibility,' he whispers as he slips the ring onto my finger. A brown buffalo cow stares at me, turning her head as we pass. Her eyes are deep and heavy and she is the next to be auctioned, along with her mate, who is chained at her side. They were sold for seven hundred dollars and their calf went to a rancher who lives a state away in Idaho.

The auctioneer begins again, calling for the highest bidder. He has a deep raucous voice and rattles off numbers as if plagued by an incurable stutter. Ernie takes me by the arm and asks once again. No, I don't want a buffalo. It would not change anything, except that we would have to find a place to park it.

Canyons gutted by rapids which fall from the mountains zip past below. Jagged cliffs of red and yellow clay rise as dark storm clouds scud across their ridges. In the distance, white vertical streaks of what must be rain meet the ground and the wind shrieks in and out of the crevasses. We are leaving the Wyoming badlands and entering a pine forest whose trees have been charred by a brush fire. Even this is a reminder. The Department of Parks in this part of the country has developed a new theory which they are experimenting with. 'Spontaneous combustion is natural, just as growth is natural,' a sign instructs us. That is why, it goes on to explain, a few miles up north twenty thousand acres of virgin timber have been smouldering since June and we can see ahead of us a thin layer of yellow-gray smoke that stretches across the sky.

To our right in a bog of weeds, an aging buffalo grazes in

solitude, knee-deep in water, his head bobbing up and down as if he had been animated for display. We pass another sign which says 'Buffalos are never seen in this area during the summer months.'

'I guess he didn't read the sign,' Ernie says, patting my thigh, as The Green Arrow, the camper we have purchased for this journey, bolts around a curve. 'What are you thinking about?'

That was the way the universe began, Ernie told me once when we lay in bed, trying to make a baby. He had read about it in *Scientific American* that afternoon. Just like it says in the Bible. First there was a void and suddenly a tremendous explosion. 'There was something when an instant before there was nothing. Science can never explain it,' he said, as we gazed at the dark, empty space between where we lay and the ceiling.

'About that sign. About what is said about spontaneous combustion,' I mumble, moving away from his patting hand and pressing myself against the window so that I can look down the sharp decline.

Being an archaeologist, I have spent the afternoon at our campsite, looking for the remnants of ancient times, signs that others were here way before ourselves. Ernie encourages me to do this because he thinks it will have a salutory effect; it has been some time since I practiced my profession in the field. This, I assume, is also part of the cure. I crawl along the ground in search of flint arrowheads, bits of hide from tepees, bows, crockery, shards, bones and scalps and trail markers. Going back further in time, into that era when glaciers carved out that choppy divide called the Rocky Mountains and the world was so icy and cold, I seek dinosaur bones, frozen mammoths, caves and cave paintings, tracings left by Cro-Magnon man. I have been trying to substantiate a theory that Ernie and I are not suited for one another because of our divergent backgrounds. He is descended from Neanderthal man because of his general clumsiness, his heavy supra-orbital ridges. I am descended from Cro-Magnon because of my more refined features and my tendency to write on bathroom walls.

Ernie, the more practical of the two of us, has been setting up camp. Reknowned eagle scout that he was in his teens, honored in six states and by the President, he has neglected to bring the tent stakes, mosquito repellent, toilet paper, and flashlight. But we are making do. There is one air mattress and tonight he wins the toss. We pass a good hour removing rocks from beneath my tarp bedding. One is shaped like a Comanche arrowhead, another like the tibiofibula of a female brontosaurus. Ernie lights the campfire and begins the cooking. He flips the hamburgers while I stir the corn.

'Once we had to set up camp in three feet of snow. It was the coldest night of any of our lives, so cold that while you slept, your breath still formed little clouds. We slept inside each other's sleeping bags and shivered all night. They called that survival training.'

We sit on the ground a few inches away from one another with the canvas of our army jackets rustling as we graze shoulders in the process of eating, the way two people on their first date might casually brush against one another to see if they'll feel that first tingle of attraction.

'When I was very small and my father took me camping, I used to be afraid of the sky. Afraid that I would see something terrible. I don't know what, something that would appear from outer space or an explosion. I read too many comic books, I guess. He told me that there was nothing to be afraid of because the stars were just lights on the crossroads where people meet.'

'Your father never liked me,' I said.

'He was very old-fashioned,' Ernie replies, looking back into the fire. I reach out for his hand as he reaches for mine and we stub fingers against one another. It has been a kind of reflex between us for some months now, since Aaron died. In the dark we seem to look for one another at exactly the same moment and there is always an elbow for an eye, two heads crashing together, a stream of 'excuse-me's, did I hurt you?'

'Is that all your father said about stars?'

'He said you should always make a wish when one shoots by.

He was a very cautious man and he hated missed opportunities. He believed you needed all the help you could get.'

Ernie tosses another log onto the fire while I lean back, waiting for some yellow streak to cut across the sky.

'You're cold,' he says, wrapping an arm around my shoulder. I ease into his arm, fit myself into the groove of his body as he slumps in front of the fire. We have been living like porcupines in winter who push close to one another to escape the cold but soon feel the prick of the other's quills. So we drift apart again until the cold is more than we can bear. And we hold one another as if we were hummingbirds whose hearts break if you grasp them ever-so-gently in the palm of your hand.

We crawl into our tent. He has forgotten to let the sleeping bags air out in the sun and they are damp inside.

'I deserve a medal for this,' I say, my teeth chattering, as I slip into my bag which is zipped against his.

'For excellence in camping skills?'

'For endurance.' I try to slip beside him on the air mattress but it is too narrow and I roll onto the ground. I look at him, floating above me like a survivor of a shipwreck on the only raft.

'Do you want the air mattress?'

'We played fair. You won the toss.'

'You'll sleep better; you need your sleep.'

He knows that as he sleeps, I will lie awake at his side. He knows that every night since last spring, I relive it; one way or another it is always there. And if I do sleep, I dream of my own self locked in small compartments of trains rushing through dark tunnels. Being buried alive through some tired intern's negligence. Trapped in a tiger cage in the confusion of a government coup, being kidnapped and stuffed in a trunk, driven two states away. I have found a book which says that 'a mother sometimes acquires the symptoms of her child' and I have consoled Ernie with the fact that when I wake up, out-of-breath, experts say this may happen. But Ernie says 'enough is enough' when I remember how I went into the bedroom and found Aaron lying so still in his crib. Ernie came upstairs after me, because he had been comforting the old woman whose kitchen had burned. 'The damage is slight,' he said. Then he saw. He acted quickly. The firemen were still downstairs and he yelled at them for their oxygen. The two events had nothing to do with one another, except they have stayed together in my mind. A crib death, the doctor said. It happens, they told me, and reminded me that he had been a weak baby at birth. A breech, like his mother.

I reach up and run my fingers over his unshaven face. The ring which we bought from the Indian makes a path through the stubble.

'Are you comfortable?'

'Are you?'

But he is tired and worn and already he is drifting off to sleep beside me. 'Being with you,' he has said, 'is like being in a room filled with people.' I tire him easily, it seems. On his air mattress, he looks so large, like a giant, from where I lie on the bumpy ground.

Outside a branch crackles; there is a rustling through a pile of leaves. Being an archaeologist, I am not uninstructed in such matters. I recognize it to be the sound of something large, mammoth, hairy which has just thawed itself out of a chunk of ice where it has slept for a hundred thousand years and promptly reproduced itself. Something groveling and wary, as if all those bones I had sought to cart away had suddenly risen up and reassembled themselves into a logical, life-giving pattern, and are slowly making their way toward us in the night.

'What was that?'

'What was what?' Ernie asks, heavy with sleep.

'That noise.'

'The wind, a deer. Nothing serious.'

He is too tired to see a glacier, purposeful and directed, creeping slowly down the mountain toward our campsite. But I am not too tired. I see the buffalo cow having broken loose from her chain, roaming the ranges in search of me to empathize with her plight. I see the clusters of stars as they burst apart and all shoot across the sky in unison and the earth as it jerks around and spins in reverse, carrying us back to a time when all was icy and cold. I see a grizzly and a deer emerge from the fire which has ignited of its own accord, which the rangers let burn while Smokey the Bear stands by, shaking a scolding finger back and forth.

'Gretchen, what's wrong? Lie still.' His fingers touch my cheek, but as I move toward them, he is asleep again. 'Babies are binding,' we said to one another when we learned we were going to have one for ourselves. But now we are like piers, reaching out across water – disappointed bridges, someone called them once.

Ernie grips my hand as the Apaches rush in. Some brave, his face painted, looking terribly mean, rides forward on his pinto and presents himself. After a brief parley in which no one seems able to reach any viable settlement, they yell and take a woman. Cochise, benevolent this time, intervenes on the part of the woman and his braves protest adamantly but it does no one any good because just at that that moment the United States Cavalry arrives.

'Tomorrow we'll go to the Buffalo Bill Museum,' he says. 'Will you like that?'

I shrug my shoulders. Ernie takes my hand and begins rubbing it, the way you rub numbness out of a frozen limb. He rubs so hard that the back of my hand begins to burn and I pull it away. He looks at the empty space where my hand has been, like an outfielder who has stretched for a fly and then watches it slip through his hands.

We leave the theater and emerge into the cool night air of Cody. I can still hear the galloping hooves as the Indians retreat in a trail of dust but it is only a few school children as they scamper down an alleyway. Ernie directs me to his old stomping ground, the Wild Stallion Saloon, where we drink beer with cowboys who are engaging in a genealogy war.

'I'm Annie Oakley's third cousin, twice removed,' says a one-armed cowboy.

'Jessie James fathered me in a Montana brothel,' another declares, drunker than the first.

As we sit by the bar, an Indian who introduces himself as Tommy Hawk sits down beside us and begins to tell the story of his life, the history of the Five Nations, the linguistic origins of the Algonquin tongue. He says that he is 120 years old, though he does not look a day over thirty and attributes his youthfulness to a steady diet of apple cider vinegar and honey. We buy him a beer and he loosens up. He gives us a detailed account of the Sioux Uprising, the Apache Migration, the life of the Plains Indians. We buy him another beer and he has the Cheyennes fighting the Apaches with phantom jets, the Comanches using antiballistic missile systems against the United States Navy. He throws some old chicken bones onto the counter and informs me obliquely that the run-away is already caught. He downs a shot of whiskey and does a fertility dance and then a rain dance 'to stop the burning in the desert and in the heart,' which is the same as his fertility dance; he says that he is an escaped convict and very dangerous. He wears purple feathers glued to his hat and carries a toy rifle, the kind every boy has when he is six years old.

We buy Tommy Hawk another beer and get up to leave the saloon. The big two-fisted cowboy, who was spawned in a Montana brothel, spits tobacco and mutters something under his breath. As we leave, the swinging doors pound gently into our backs.

We have spent the day climbing with Ernie leading the way. This is his territory; he knows it well. When he was a boy, he followed this path to the lake at its top called the Mystic where he used to fish with his father. I like the name. It reminds me of something cool and refreshing and the day is hot and muggy. Ernie says that it is like going back to the source, climbing to this lake again. He says it is like coming home after being away for a long time and working very hard because it is difficult to be home at first when you're tired and nervous and unaccustomed, but soon you relax and it begins to heal that part of you that has been working too hard. He says it will be better when we reach the top. We can swim and sleep in the sun and make men out of the snow that still lies on the ground. We have been climbing for several hours now and I am annoying him by continuing to search the ground for artifacts of lost civilizations, including one pair of human footprints which I have followed until they led me directly back to Ernie.

We reach the last steep climb before the divide and he has to pull me up. I imagine that, as he stretches down to help me, the trail suddenly gives way and from where I stand I can see him tumbling over and over, down into that deep canyon, and I can do nothing but listen to him calling and watch the rocks crashing over the spot where he has just fallen.

'Don't look down,' he warns. 'Look up, this way.' As I lean forward, reaching for his hand, I see his eyes. They are opened wide, almost bulging, and his mouth is gaping, like a fish out of water gasping for air, and even though he is smiling, I see that he is afraid of letting go of me as well. At level ground we fall into each other's arms and he presses me so tightly against him that I feel all my bones cracking back into place.

As we begin our descent to the lake, we notice a yellow-gray layer of smoke rising against the sky and a group of rangers in khaki-colored trousers ordering us back. The fire has reached the lake. We can go no further, their signals tell us. But Ernie refuses to believe them. We have, after all, been climbing all day. He goes up to where a ranger is standing. 'What do you mean, we can't go ahead?' He protests that he knows this terrain, he comes from here. He points an angry finger in the direction of Mystic Lake. 'We aren't going to where the fire is.' He is shouting at the ranger now. I look away, pretending I am not with him, but we are the only two people on this side of the mountain, except for the rangers, and so it is useless to pretend. His face is turning red as if he is warm and the ranger argues that at any moment the wind could shift, the fire could move to the other side of the lake. Ernie shakes his head and tells the ranger it's the dumbest argument he's ever heard. 'How can a fire cross water?' Ernie demands to know.

'Mister,' the ranger shakes his head, 'you'd be surprised.'

I touch Ernie by the sleeve and tell him that I don't really want to go where the fire is. Already the smoke is bringing tears to my eyes. I have no interest in watching acres of virgin forest burn. But Ernie doesn't even see the fire. All he sees are his father and himself, knee-deep in water, waiting for trout. He stares despondently at the lake, as if it were some toy he'd always wanted, as if the ranger and his rules were somehow taking his childhood away.

Ernie looks back at the ranger and the ranger, who is finally beginning to lose patience, looks at Ernie. Below, where the lake is, billows of smoke rise. We can see fire fighters, madly digging ditches, trying to keep the fire in one place. The fire suddenly seems enormous to me, bigger than us all, as if just for the fun of it, the fire would hurdle those ditches, work its way around the lake, encircle us.

Ernie is still trying to reason with the ranger. 'If it won't cross the ditches, it certainly won't cross the lake, right?'

The ranger nods, obviously bored by these city slickers who think they know everything. I begin taking the ranger's side. 'The wind could easily shift,' I hear myself saying. 'We'd be trapped in there.'

'Mister, your wife has the right idea. Now why don't you people just go back to your campsite and come back in a few days.'

Ernie shouts at the ranger as I pull him away. 'You don't understand, do you? I grew up here.' I'm tugging at his arm, nodding apologies at the ranger who has in some way become my ally. Ernie is angry at both of us now but finally he gives up and lets me lead him away, as dejected as an actor who has just ruined his scene.

Ernie takes my hand and it seems to disappear in his as we begin the long trudge back to camp. He curses the ranger, the United States Forest Service, the Department of Parks. His anger doesn't even seem to have much to do with the fire and the ranger. He is just angry. It is rare that he wants something he can't have. Everything has always come easily his way.

As we cross back to the trail, I pause and look back toward the mountains. Ernie, who is talking about writing a letter to Mike Mansfield, momentarily forgetting that the senior senator from Montana has long since retired, pauses and looks back as well. Suddenly there appears, standing motionless on the top of a butte, a brilliant orange – the buffalo cow in flames, scanning the valley with her lonesome eyes.

On Borrowed Time

***

W HEN I MOVED into the second floor of a five-story walk-up, they told me that the second floor was better than the first because a burglar would have to bring a ladder into the garden and not many burglars would go to that trouble. But the previous tenant confided in me. She had been robbed while she slept. She was a light sleeper so the burglars must have been very considerate. I felt assured. I am a light sleeper too.

The man from 2F watched as movers dragged my sofa vertically up the narrow stairwell. When they left, he came inside unannounced with two mugs. 'Sugar?' he asked, sitting on a carton across from me. 'My name's Bradley. Bradley Roundtree.' He extended his hand and I shook it. Then he passed a mug of coffee. 'You should feel honored,' he said. 'Heat shortage, coffee shortage, and you've got both. Beginner's luck. I'm mostly Cheyenne Indian, do you believe that?' I nodded; I had no reason to doubt him. 'My father was a brave. When he was fifteen, he fought at the Battle of the Little Big Horn. I may not look it but I'm almost fifty. I was the first Indian dancer with the New York City Ballet. You didn't know they had Indian dancers, did you? Most of them are crazy. Sometimes I wish I'd stayed on the reservation.' He rose suddenly and leaned over me. 'I talk too much and you've got all these things to take care of. If you need anything, just holler.'

He left as abruptly as he'd arrived, disappearing into his

apartment. He forgot to take his mug and it would be weeks before I'd remember to return it. When he left, I wandered through a maze of cartons down the hallway into the kitchen, which looks out over the garden. It was winter and the garden was under heavy snow. A light shone from a tree and the snow glistened. Then I saw another light and something I hadn't seen before. A protective house of glass, like a greenhouse, only it shimmered under the ice like an igloo or a palace of crystal. I fumbled through the cartons for the binoculars which my previous living companion had left when he moved out. Then I saw. It wasn't a greenhouse or an igloo. It was a small glass structure, containing tanks of tropical fish. It was an emerald-green kingdom, divided by little silver darts, and laced with blue and yellow stripes. I saw gold flickers and something lavender which turned a vibrant green as it swam past the light.

It's true what they say, about walls having ears and being paper thin. My pipes rattle to the rhythm of ancient drums. To bones in the closet. A tribe lives in the walls; their messages tapped in code reveal secrets. A cult of darkness. My radiator sounds like somebody's crying. Lately, it's been imitating the buzzer, so when the heat goes on at five in the morning I rush to answer the door. No one's there. Real privacy is impossible in this house. It's like living with a family you never see. I only know what I hear. Fights between two people somewhere in the upper reaches travel through my vents. Clock radios go off and I know who's waking by the music. Bradley wakes at seven and does calisthenics to WRVR. I feel the vibrations of his push-ups under the bed. At seven-thirty, Mrs. Wendell, who I've learned from Bradley is a widow and mother of the fish, rises to 'the mellow sound' of FM 92. She checks the temperature on the outdoor tanks and turns on the Today Show which I get in my bathroom. I've yet to see the man from 3R but he calls out names in the night. Maybe he's the one who leaves a carnation in my mailbox slot every Monday morning. Bradley says it's been going on for years and used to drive the previous tenant crazy too. The old couple in 4R get up at eight to a Latin station and their dog barks until they take it out. I don't know how they make it up the stairs. Only Estelle, the frail woman in 1F below me who has a mysterious disease, never makes a sound; sometimes I press my ear to the floor for some sign that she's there.

It's the worst winter I can recall. Two nights ago a freezing cold rain fell and turned to snow and beneath the snow there is ice. I've worried about the fish since it rained. Then last night, returning from grocery shopping, I saw Pedro Mansillas, the old man from the fourth floor, coming down the stairs. I was on the sidewalk when he slipped, almost in slow motion, his mouth rounded in a pout. Then he let out a cry which came after he had reached the ground. When I rushed to help, he stared at me. He wasn't hurt but there was a look of terror in his eyes, as if he'd seen a ghost.

'Any fool can see a brownstone like this wouldn't have an elevator,' the man from 5F said when I opened the door. 'Maggie saw it and swore there was an elevator, but there isn't.' He paused and smiled. He was tall and broad with a reddish beard and a fading tan. 'Would you believe,' he said, extending a cup my way, 'I'd like to borrow some sugar. I just can't bear going out in this weather and I can't get a thing done without coffee.' I took his cup and filled it with sugar. Then I offered him a cup of coffee which I'd just brewed. 'You're new,' he said, slumping into an armchair and putting his feet on the table, 'and you're the only one home, at least as far down as I went. Maybe the old people are in but they aren't answering. They have a canary record they play all day long.' I nodded; I got the canary in the kitchen. He sipped on his coffee. 'I suppose the walk-up is good for me. My father died at forty-five.' He didn't look like someone who had to worry about premature death. 'Maybe we could work out a self-help system. I hate running to the store for a Coke.'

His name was Stephen Woodring and he lived with a woman named Maggie Jacobs who was looking for another apartment because they weren't getting along and it was just a matter of time before one would throw the other out. 'We fight about everything now. You name it; we'll fight about it.'

'I know,' I mumbled. He looked surprised so I had to explain that I could hear it through the vent in the living room.

'You must have a good ear.'

I nodded and was glad I didn't have to explain that most of my income came from composing jingles for bathroom cleanser. I was relieved when he went on how it was a long story about him and Maggie. 'She never talks about anything,' he said, 'and she never knows what the hell she wants. Eating in a Chinese restaurant is impossible with her because she never makes a decision.' Her first decision in years, it seems, was to come live with Stephen. Her second was to leave. He had dark eyes and ran his hand absently through a head of thick curls. In general, he was fed up. It'd cost him a thousand dollars to move his upright piano through a fifth story window so he could get a little relaxation. 'Do you play?'

'A little,' I nodded.

'Well, feel free to use it any time you want when she's not around.' He'd wanted to be a concert pianist but his father insisted on a responsible career. He still played, mostly jazz, mostly improvised.

'Where're you from?'

'The Midwest.'

'Horses?' He seemed to perk up.

'We had dozens of horses.'

When he was a boy, he'd had a pink horse that went everywhere with him. Actually it was red and white but from a distance of ten feet it was pink. 'If I wasn't riding him, he walked behind me. You'd be surprised how loyal a horse can be. Oh, yeah, I forgot. You had horses. But we were inseparable.' He'd grown up in Brazil where his father worked for an oil company. Then one day the horse wandered too close to the jungle and was eaten by a mountain lion. He snapped his fingers to show me how fast it had happened.

He needed some other things and handed me his shopping

list. After two hours, he left with the sugar, a can of olives, my stapler, and a bar of Ivory soap.

Bradley told me the man above me who calls names in the night is an astronomer who works at the planetarium around the corner. He believes apples always fall at the same rate, no matter where you plant the tree. He also thinks the Roman Empire would have declined at the same speed on Mars. 'A deranged scientist,' Bradley said. 'At night you can catch him staring at the sky. A real weirdo.' Bradley reviews with me the state of affairs in the building when he comes to fix the faucet, which is often. Pedro was lucky not to break his hip when he fell. The landlord from Sicily has an altar to Buffalo Bill and shoots clay pigeons in a sound-proof basement. Estelle is in remission from a disease that keeps the iron floating aimlessly in her veins, never resting in the cells. The lady with the fish is a witch. This is the third time he's had to fix the faucet. At night it drips steadily, no matter what I do to stop it, and the dripping penetrates pipes stuffed with cotton and closed doors.

'I see Stephen and Maggie are going at it again.' He gave the wrench a sharp twist to the right. 'Oh . . .' I was trying to hold the faucet in place.

'The landlord should really do something about this.' Bradley frowned at the sink. 'They've been having trouble since they moved in. You should hear the shouting. I've seen him coming down to see you lately.' I told him Stephen only comes when he needs something. Bradley gave one more sharp turn of the wrench and removed the old washer which he tossed into the garbage. 'That's shot.' Then he fumbled in his tool kit for a new one. 'Why aren't you married?

'I was.' Actually, I wasn't but I lived with a man for a few years who walked out when I was at work and left me a check for two months rent. Bradley handed me the wrench and showed me how to fix the faucet.

'The sink's shot,' he said. 'Petition for a new one.' When he left, I placed the wrench on the shelf next to his mug.

'I seeya spenda time widda Mista Woodring. Datsa good cuz he'sa nica man and datta woman donna know a good tin when she gottit,' my landlady said when she came to inspect the spot. It had been growing like a nebula on the ceiling where the astronomer, watching the stars, forgot to watch his bath. It's a large blotch and the plaster comes down in huge chunks which crash in the the night. First Bradley inspected the damage. I've seen a lizard and an angel in the spot so far but Bradley doesn't care if I see the sugar plum fairy because it's going to get a lot worse before it gets better. We have to wait until the plaster dries, which can take weeks, before the landlord can redo it. The astronomer claims he doesn't know how it happened and Stephen'll handle the case for free if I have to sue. The landlady says they ainta gonna pay notting and the astronomer says the pipes've been useless since he can remember.

But the fact is, the place is falling apart. I've learned a lot since I got here. A burglar wouldn't need a ladder to reach my window and the previous tenant was raped. Hot water never gets to the top floor and heat doesn't leave the bottom. Estelle, whom I've never seen, complains to the landlord about the noise I make walking across the floor. It's so cold the windows have frozen shut and I can't see outside. It's been a long time since I saw the fish but I stopped worrying because their house is heated. Bradley gets depressed if there's nothing for him to repair. Stephen has compiled a long list of what he owes me. Lately I've been running errands through the snow for Ruth, Pedro's wife.

When the buzzer rang in the middle of the night, I thought it was the radiator. When it rang again, I went to the door. Stephen leaned against the doorway, bleary-eyed. He said it was important or he'd never come at this hour. 'I just don't know who to turn to,' he said. Maggie was packing. 'Believe me, I've tried everything, everything.' He sank down on the sofa.

'Where's she going to go on a freezing cold night at two in the morning?' I said.

He dropped his face into his hands. 'We're just basically incompatible.' He rubbed his eyes with his hands. 'My parents are professional; hers are working class. She can't cope with ambition; I hate penny-pinching. If I'm hot, she's absolutely lifeless. It goes on and on.' When I told him I wished I had his problems, he stared at me in disbelief. 'I left my wife for this woman. Now she's leaving me. And I'm keeping you up at all hours. There's no justice.'

I made a pot of tea and Stephen sipped his from Bradley's mug. Walking to the window, I remembered a night when I returned to an empty apartment. 'She's probably in bed,' I said, 'waiting for you to get back upstairs.'

'You think so?' He seemed incredulous.

I nodded but the truth was I hoped she'd left. The next day Stephen called me to thank me for my help and to tell me how happy he was because Maggie wasn't going to leave after all.

Mrs. Wendell, the fish lady, was thrilled when she caught me. She poised her bulk in the hallway, nervously rubbing her hands. Then she led me through an array of plants sprouting from old shoes, newspapers from last August, a pile of logs, fish nets, a barbecue, music boxes which she wound as she passed them, a blackbird who sang 'Good night, Ladies,' a scattering of undergarments and petticoats, flung at random around the room. I followed as she carved a path through the kitchen, forged a passageway among the soiled dishes, shelves lined with seaweed, fish food, plastic toys for the aquariums, cat boxes, and suitcases which were bulging and stuffed to go nowhere. She opened the door which led to the garden and snow whirled in front of us. She flicked the light and the garden was illuminated as we dashed through the snow. Inside the glass house, an orange tree was thriving beside a dwarfed cocoanut palm. She tapped her fingers on the tanks, reviving sleeping catfish, plump sea horses, fish that bared their teeth.

Then she told me in detail the history of each fish. The zebra fish was from Bengal and she'd ridden through a jungle for it. The white cloud was smuggled out of Canton while the pearl gourami with its vibrant purple once swam in a mosaic pool before secret altars in Cambodia. She'd journeyed to Borneo for one, to Panama for another. She pointed to a five-inch long goldfish, cruising a labyrinth of plastic with its scrawny mate. 'Goldie's thirty-five,' she said, leading me back out into the snow. 'They live to be very old if you take good care of them. He was my first fish.'

I stomped the snow from my shoes as she put on a kettle for tea. 'Why do you keep them outside?'

She shrugged her shoulders. 'Always have. No room for them inside with all this junk.' She pointed to all the corners of the room, to the unhung portraits of ancestors on the floor. We sat down in the living room in her overstuffed armchairs, sipping herbal tea which she claimed had medicinal powers. 'I know what you need,' she said, laughing a short laugh. 'I understand women.' I took a good look at her. She was yellow and ugly and fragile and I believed her.

At night there's a new sound. A man's footsteps. They moved back and forth high above me and I knew that sound because it was once familiar to me. It's the sound of coming home to everything changed. Maggie, whom I never did meet, after weeks of threats and packing, moved out abruptly the same week Estelle told the landlord to tell me not to wear shoes.

It was a long time before I saw Stephen again and when I did, he was bundled up, muffler, gloves, hiking boots, ready to traverse the Yukon. 'Where's your dog sled?' I said. He was going to walk to the new Egyptian wing at the museum across the park and wanted me to join him. We huddled against the cold, leaving stark tracks, walked on a frozen lake which gave out a loud, cracking sound as we stood in the middle. On the other side we unburied a sign which read 'thin ice.' A vagabond shivered beneath a tree and we gave him a dollar even though he wasn't asking. Stephen had brought a dried roll which we crunched up and fed to the animals. I waited but he didn't say a word about Maggie. The wind was at our faces but going home we'd have it at our backs.

When we arrived, we entered the tomb. Stephen touched the

old walls and perused the engravings while I tried to decipher symbols. The jaguar, the scarab, the crocodile. He stared into an empty mummy case and at hieroglyphics from the *Book of the Dead*. We learned from a guide who offered a free explanation how in Egypt each body awaited and came prepared for a reunion with its lost soul. On the way back, the wind was in our faces again.

It was dark and the snow was deep. Someone whizzed by on an American flyer sled. Stephen, beaming with liberation, suddenly wanted to build what he called a snowperson. I packed a small head while he worked on the base. While he worked on the torso, I flopped down and made three snow angels. 'That's amazing.' He pointed at the angels. 'They look just like real ones.' Then he flopped down and tried one himself while I tried to raise the torso onto the base. Stephen caught me from behind and dragged me down into the snow with him. I fought until we were both covered with a coating of powder. 'I can't stop laughing,' Stephen said as we searched for objects with which to sculpt a face. We put branches like antlers on the head of the snowperson, stone eyes far back on the head and looking at the sky, watching for snow, an E-Z Wider rolled cigarette without tobacco stuffed into a hand-carved mouth.

It seems I've always lived in winter. I remember the desolate reaches of white terrain more than I remember the ice breaking or planting in spring. Hot chocolate was always waiting in a pot on the stove. It took me years to learn to use the back door in winter and put everything in the mud closet before coming in. Stephen took me by the arm but I was hesitant to move on. Somehow he must have sensed it because he packed more snow at the base of our snowperson, whom we named Alfred Beatrice after two polar bear cubs I once saw incubated in a Chicago zoo. They were tiny, like rabbits. I was sad as we waved goodbye and wended our way through the park. Small lights lit the paths like gas lanterns but the wind was still in our faces and we walked with our eyes half shut. Stephen wrapped an arm across my shoulder and I leaned against him. 'I don't want you blowing away,' he said.

The five-story walk-up was more tiring than the walk through the snow. I had to rest on the third landing. Stephen raced up the stairs ahead of me. Once inside he built a small fire in his working fireplace. 'I know it pollutes,' he muttered, 'but once in a while we're entitled.' I played the 'Moonlight Sonata' while he brewed Irish coffee. While we drank the coffee, Stephen played adaptations from Charlie Parker with one hand. Then he served a liquor brewed from a berry indigenous only to the north of Finland, cloudberry. My lids grew heavy and I lay back in front of the fire on the sofa. Stephen put a pillow under my head and another on the back of the sofa. He leaned against it staring into the fire.

'Mind if I stay here?' I mumbled, half asleep. Stephen yawned, sat upright.

'You mean all night?' I nodded with my eyes closed. He sat forward to the edge of the sofa. 'Well, sure, if you're too tired to go back downstairs.' I opened my eyes and saw him heading for his bedroom to bring me a blanket.

'No, it's O.K.' I rose from the sofa. 'I'll be better off in my own bed.' He put the blanket back on his bed and came back, visibly relieved. I remembered how it took time, when you're back on your own. At the door I kissed him on the cheek but he seemed to pull away as if wounded. I clomped down the stairs while he yawned and waved good-bye.

My brother got a detailed report. He listened with care, clicked his teeth from his apartment near the garment district, and said, 'Wear pink.' I didn't understand. 'You know, pink like cotton candy.' The only pink article of clothing in my wardrobe was a terry cloth beach robe, long-sleeved, which dragged on the floor and looked like a tent.

'Did I get you out of the shower?' Stephen glanced at his watch. 'Maybe I'm early.' I rubbed my arms in the beach robe and complained about the heat. The lights were low. Chick Corea improvisations were on the stereo and Stephen paused, as he walked across the room, to listen to them. He'd brought his cloudberry down with him but we began with double scotches.

Soon he was a teenager, transplanted from Brazil to New Jersey, ensconced in adolescent misery and earnest rebellion. He'd tried to drown his incurable loneliness in the bodies of women, behind the factories of Bayway, women who followed him in his army jacket from drunken parties to the seclusion of the parks, the woman he made love to on a lunch counter when he had a summer job at Grant's. Then one day it all stopped because he was harboring an empty spot deep inside. He paused and was silent. 'I don't know why I'm telling you all this stuff.' He cleared his throat and stared ahead of him, as if watching a procession pass. When he went to fix another drink, I was ready to reach out and touch him.

He was almost sitting back down when the doorbell rang. 'Excuse me,' a faint, woman's voice said over the intercom, 'but I used to live here and was coming back to pick up some things; I don't seem to have the downstairs key.' A pale, lanky woman with limbs like a praying mantis made her way up the stairs. Her earth shoes were noiseless. Tiny breasts were revealed through her transparent shirt, visible when her pea coat parted. 'Thanks. Hope I didn't get you up.' She glanced at my beach robe. 'I'm Maggie Jacobs.'

I shook her hand feebly and her hand in mine was like a dead fish. Stephen sank into the sofa but didn't disappear. When she saw him, she didn't flinch. 'Nice place you've got here.' She nodded at Stephen who fidgeted nervously. He rose to go upstairs with her and she stood in the doorway nonchalantly, like a Sherman tank. He said he'd be back as soon as he could. I slammed the door and changed into jeans and a denim shirt.

The phone rang. 'She's tearing the place apart,' he said. I sat down with old magazines to wait. The phone rang again. It was a man who I'd been seeing occasionally for a few weeks, an investigative reporter. He was the kind who always said 'hi' when you answered the phone and never gave his name, as if recognizing his voice proved some form of intimacy. I always said 'Who is this?' to show he had no place in my life. When not delving into the latest horror story, he meditated in front of a picture of his swami from Tibet. While he meditated, his

Stouffer's dinner would heat in the oven. He was a man who seemed capable of lurid, private acts. On our first date, he asked if I knew Stephen Woodring, an attorney who lived in my building. He said he was involved in all sorts of graft.

'She left like a beggar lady. Two shopping bags.' I was trying to understand what he saw in her. 'I never wanted her to leave.' he said, dropping his head into his hands.

'You're better off without her. She hates men.'

'How can you tell?' I shrugged my shoulders but my words had reassured him. Already he was seeing new women. The artist who does mechanicals for *Family Circle*. The paralegal with the husky. He was optimistic about everything.

'I'm seeing a famous investigative reporter,' I told him, hoping to provoke curiosity.

'There's one of those guys whose trying to make me into a crook. You know,' he sat forward, 'I know what I want. If I saw it, I'd know it.' He poured the last two shots of cloudberry. The name made me sleepy. I saw men in Finland in reindeer suits, knee-deep in snow, picking berries from bushes. I wanted to go to Finland and join them. As I moved closer to him, he stretched, said he had to be up early, and in a few moments was gone.

A blue diamond lights up the naked shrubs in the garden, shimmers on the branches still golden brown and now, deep in the garden, violet and crimson, flashes of copper, the tropics flourish, barely understood. Below there are divers off the reefs while fish in water scull through hoops of coral. Some would think it a rain forest or a travel poster. The frost has cleared and from the window stars can be seen, shining remote as colored fishes. Goldie swims beside his scrawny mate. Polaris to the north, Venus on the horizon, the bright morning star, Orion, Mars, the Bears surround the moon in a misty circle which forebodes more snow. If you look carefully, there are the Pleiades in Taurus, Andromeda in the northern constellations, south of Cassiopeia. A cat scurries past, chased by another; yellow eyes look up, glimmering in the light hung from the magnolia tree.

Once they said a great comet would come ripping out of the

sky and I waited the whole month of July but nothing came until I finally spotted a tiny star with a tiny white tail like a rabbit. That's when I decided nothing spectacular happens out there, except for a rare eclipse, a brief shooting star. But mostly it's predictable, not particularly given to change. I waited for weeks for that comet but in the end all we got was a lesson in continuity. Lives, I figured from the vantage point of a Nebraska cornfield, were like the invisible lines we'd imagined as the tails of comets. If they met, the crossroads would be lit by stars, brief flickers in the blackness of night.

Mrs. Wendell brought me a portrait of one of her uncles which I hung over the mantel. He wore a frilly blue blouse and had committed suicide at the age of twenty-six for unexplained reasons, though the family suspected illicit love. Pedro and Ruth sat in front of the building on folding chairs in the sun and assessed the weather with everyone who passed. Bradley met a woman by answering a personal ad and they fell in love. She had pasty white skin and long red nails. He fixed my ceiling himself and Stephen went with me to small claim's court when the landlord refused to pay. We lost the case before a judge who Stephen swore had mafia connections, along with the landlord. The investigative reporter told me he'd proved conclusively that Stephen wasn't ripping off old people and I told him 'of course not' and wouldn't see him again. The astronomer announced to everyone he met on the stairs that he'd seen pictures of a huge mountain range on Mars and that it was obvious from the slopes of the ridges that the range was filled with gold.

Stephen went to Caracas on business and sent me a postcard, every word of which I analyzed as if it were written in the secret language of spies. Was he really sleeping under mosquito netting when he wrote it? Was it romantic, camping by the Rio de Madre? There was no mention of business. I had the piano tuner come in and I watered the plants while he was away. Some nights I just sat at the piano. One night I got drunk and composed a one and a half minute jazz number which I dedicated to Stephen called 'Snow Angels.'

'Play it again,' he said. He lay with his feet up on the sofa.

For the third time I played 'Snow Angels' for him. He seemed to like it. 'I brought you a present,' he said. Undoing his suitcase, which he hadn't yet unpacked, he brought out an Indian hat, made out of llama fur, with a squared forehead and long, flopping ears. I put it on and looked ridiculous. He said it was from Peru.

'It's very nice. I thought you went to Caracas.'

'I moved around a bit.'

I took off the hat, which I never wore again, and sat down on the sofa beside him. We were drinking double scotches again. It seemed whenever we were together, we were drinking. But with Stephen, the more he drank, the more he talked. He made a space on the sofa and told me about the whores of Caracas. They played musical instruments from the hidden recesses of alleyways. Strange bewitching melodies on instruments he couldn't name. Once he followed a haunting melody until he found himself face-to-face with a diseased, painted prune.

He sighed. 'Caracas isn't the same. It's like New Jersey.' It was all the back of the factory again. It was capitalism and Mr. Taco. 'We're living in a take-out, freeze-dried world and we better get used to it.' It wasn't difficult for me to lean over and kiss him on the lips, a brief kiss which was not returned. For the first time, the building was quiet. Suddenly there wasn't a taxi honking, a traffic jam or emergency anywhere in the city. Stephen gaped at me.

'I want you,' I said very softly.

Stephen laughed nervously, 'I want a lot of things I can't have,' he replied, shaking his head. 'Your timing's just off a little.'

He suddenly got an evil look in his eyes, or at least he seemed to, as if there were something extremely sly about him, too sly to ever be considered shallow. Or perhaps that somewhat detached smile, those eyes that would not look at me, were just things I imagined in my own hunger. I thought of the nights I'd pictured him with Maggie. They were wild beasts, harsh and beyond control. We weren't going to be that way. We'd have an Irish setter and do crosswords and somehow we wouldn't be bored. 'I thought you liked me,' I said. 'I thought when we went out in the snow that you were interested and it was just a matter of time.'

I waited for him to grasp that I felt led on, abused, though when I thought about it, he'd never really made pretenses of being anything other than my friend. I felt completely ashamed; the power people have when they reject us is terrible. Stephen reached for his drink and seemed ready to forget the fact that I'd made a pass at him. He brushed it off with, 'It's O.K. kid.' He sipped his drink, 'You're probably just horny. How long's it been?' It was as if someone else spoke through his lips. Before either of us knew what was happening, I was up and heading to the door. I was thinking of shouting something to him from the doorway but actually there was nothing to say. The only thing left was to leave. As I ran down the stairs which spiraled before me, I heard Stephen calling from the landing, 'Hey, look, I'm sorry; I didn't mean that,' his words following me, echoing and reverberating through the fragile walls.

As his words diminished into a blur of sound, I thought about the fragile walls. About how easily sounds pass through them. How much more penetrable they seemed than any of the people who lived in them. I decided to burn them down. At that moment it was the only real solution, the only thing I wanted to do. It would keep us from having to return all the things we couldn't return. I'd take kerosene and sprinkle it along the stairs as if I were watering them. I'd start at Stephen's door and work my way down and when I reached the bottom landing, I'd throw in the match. It seemed so logical and I might even have done it if I hadn't felt, suddenly, as if my own conscience were watching me. It was pressed against the peephole of 4R, in the shape of an eye watching me, and in Pedro Mansillas' stare was the same dark fear, the same terrible shame, I'd seen when he slipped, leaving his own fortuitous snow angel, shaken and crumpled, in the snow.

Among the Cuban Refugees

❧ ❧

I WORK IN A television studio, producing documentaries for children's programs. I have been responsible for 'Sidney, Child of the Slums,' 'A Road Taken: The Life of Robert Frost,' 'Nation of Immigrants,' and 'Animals of the American Wilderness.' In 'Animals of the American Wilderness,' a mountain lion befriends an orphaned rabbit and it had taken a year to keep the lion from eating the rabbit. During that year my husband and I separated. He was a microbiologist in charge of a swamp. I met him when I did my first documentary, 'The Hidden World,' in which he said that microbes were the original workers of the earth. Once I visited the swamp where he worked. By day it was murky and humid but at night it was suddenly transformed. Fireflies illumined the rushes while green phosphorescent specks shimmered on the surface of the water and the muddy bank. The tracks of indeterminate animals glowed along these banks as the water soaked in and filled them.

I was beginning work on the Spanish Harlem series, months behind schedule, when I looked up from my desk one day and saw a young man sprawled before me. He was pale and thin in the leather armchair and he startled me because I hadn't heard a sound when he came in. For a long time we stared at one another. His eyes, like his hair, were a shade of sullen brown. He wore a buttonless shirt safety-pinned together and black hairs waved in circles on his chest. His jeans were ancient, his white sneakers riddled with holes. An army jacket lay across his left arm which crossed his right and beneath the jacket a dark, pigmented birthmark, partially visible, covered his forearm. He scanned the graphics on my wall and dusted the leather armchair when he rose. He looked detached, almost bored, and his look expressed how I had been feeling for many months, since my husband left. I felt a strange complicity. I read his name from the card he handed to me – José Nestor Ruiz Villegas de Cordoba – and he corrected my Spanish pronunciation.

He was a free-lance animator. He said he could make anything move and he flapped his arms like a bird. I wasn't looking for an animator yet on the Spanish Harlem series and I was busy and told him he'd have to make an appointment. But he held up a demonstration reel and said it would only take a minute. In the projection room, I watched a magenta sand fly do an ad for Don Q rum, a cockroach fall in love with a mouse who died tumbling into the bouillabaisse, the Walrus and the Carpenter walking the briny beach.

José rewound the reel and looked at me. He seemed very young and slovenly. I had no way of knowing if he was reliable. It seemed certain he was not. If I looked carefully, I saw that he was beautiful, but I would try to overlook that. He folded his arms, waiting for me to decide. I hired him on the spot because he was the best animator I ever saw and a Cuban refugee.

José paced, pencil in mouth, at the drawing board across the hall. He tapped his fingers on the window as if trying to signal to someone, yawned, stretched, then flung himself onto his desk. He went into fits of drawing, tearing up what he didn't like, muttering to himself, refusing to be disturbed. He'd arrive at noon and call me at midnight to say he couldn't finish ten more drawings before the next day. Then he was at his desk before the custodians arrived and he didn't look up until everyone started to leave. It seemed he never ate, slept, or had any money. Whatever he earned, he sent home to his family or spent on flowers for his coworkers. He always left the office on foot, never took a taxi or a subway, and he had no address that could be called permanent. He said he stayed with 'friends' who seemed to be scattered throughout the city. He drank rum when it was offered and had a nervous habit of tugging on the safety pin which held each of his three shirts together.

My husband was a dark, brooding man and the friction of passion grew from our differences. Perhaps the greatest problem between us was that I'd really loved him, as much as you can love a man who doesn't speak about himself but who every day for the first year of our courtship brought me a red matador rose. It seemed that all I'd ever wanted was strange men, bizarre situations. I knew that I was very drawn to José and I also knew that I didn't need another dark stranger in my life. All day long I found excuses for going into his office. It seemed I wanted to see him all the time, yet I didn't want him to notice. Each morning and evening I went to check on his progress. Before going in I made certain I looked my best and reviewed my simple set of instructions. Avoid all eye contact. If he stares at you, stare at someone else, preferably another employee. If his work is sloppy or late, fire him on the spot. They were easy rules which I followed during his first three days at work. 'Why don't you relax?' he said without looking up from his drawing board. 'We'll never get anything done this way.'

Though he rarely spoke unless I addressed him, he was always willing to talk about Cuba. His father had worked with Castro and shared an office with Ché. 'Ché was asthmatic,' he told me. 'He had terrible attacks in the jungle but he went on fighting.' He was restless and in the middle of talking pointed to a post-card on my wall. 'Who do you know in Nazaré?' he asked. I stared at the postcard which consisted of a cliff, a strip of beach, water, and a row boat.

'How do you know it's Nazaré?' I asked.

He said he recognized the cliff formations. 'My father was a pacifist,' he said, switching back to the Revolution. 'When it got bloody, we fled.' They left Cuba on a raft made of cocoanut shells. 'We drifted for nine days,' he told me, 'and ran out of food on the fourth. We had to drink our own urine on the sixth.

When the Coast Guard picked us up, we were as good as dead.'

After five weeks, he presented his first complete set of drawings. Thirty seconds of animation for a street scene of the old city of San Juan. Women in floral dresses stood surrounding a statue of a man whose hand was pointing. Men sat at the base of the statue. Children played ball in the square. As he flipped the pages, the women strutted, the men called to them. The ball rolled out of the page and pigeons soared from the head of the statue.

When I told him the drawings were good, he asked me out for Saturday night. I remember how he was at that moment. Standing back, hands in his pockets, a half-smile on his lips. I leaned forward and studied the drawings again. 'I'm sorry,' I said, 'but I've got other plans.' On a slip of paper he wrote down the name of a club, an address, a time – 'after ten.'

'It's not a date,' he said. 'I just thought you might want to get out and hear some music.' I repeated that I was busy and told him what miniscule changes I wanted incorporated into the drawings. He listened and, without another word, left my office.

I descended the steps of El Batey, 'the slave's quarters,' on Saturday night and entered the dingy, airless room where dancers glided to the rhumba of the congos. When I was a child, we had a gardener who was Cuban and he told me about the sound of the congos. I followed him while he tended the garden and told me about how the drums can be so loud and go on for so long that the dancers stumble home in the morning with them still ringing in their ears. During the Cuban Revolution, he ran off with the maid next door and I thought all that upheaval had been caused by their elopement. I stood alone on the bottom step, staring at the dancers who would keep hearing the drums after they'd stopped.

I was about to leave when a man at the door asked if he could help. 'I'm looking for José,' I said. He disappeared into the kitchen and returned with a short, fat Puerto Rican with grease on his apron who seemed to be the cook. 'Not that one,' I said.

'Oh, you mean the musician,' and he went away again, bringing me a tall, swarthy man carrying a flute. I shook my head.

'Well, look for yourself.' I elbowed my way past apologetic dancers and carved a path through the room. I stared from table to table until I spotted the hands flung into the air, the inimitable slump, hidden behind a pole in the far corner of the room.

'So you decided to come.' He stood up.

I shrugged my shoulders. 'My plans got changed.' He nodded and introduced me to his friends, which seemed to be most of the people in the room. We danced the samba out of step, stomping on each other's toes. Walking home in the pale morning light, I touched the strange scale on his arm. 'What's that?' I asked, all tact relinquished to rum and fatigue. José explained that in his mother's womb there had been a twin who exploded and left his cells all over Jose's arm. I stared at the birthmark, seeing arms, legs, a tiny heart, the way one finds dinosaurs in the clouds. 'Does it bother you?'

He smiled the first smile I'd noticed from behind his beard. 'I'm never alone,' he said, taking me by the arm.

Cuba is an island surrounded by a maze of islets and keys. In order to come to the innermost reaches of this distant land, you must wend your way through thousands of island canals. My street seemed to become like one of those canals. My apartment became an outpost on the trail between San Juan and Boston, between Miami and New Hampshire. They made their way to my door, camped in the living room, smoked cigars, and threatened me with the overthrow of Domino Sugar. I had always wanted to travel. Now it seemed I could do so by staying at home. José gave my address to everyone and people tried to reach him through me. An uncle José didn't remember arrived from Texas. There was someone's brother and a woman who had had a part in a John Ford film. A young girl who seemed relieved when I told her José didn't live here but just used the address.

The next day, after the girl came by, I asked José to live with me. I didn't want him for my lover but I suppose I wanted a companion, someone to come home to. My husband's presence still lingered in the rooms like a ghost. The spare room which José was to occupy provided us with a safe distance, letting us ignore our arms brushing in corridors, shoulders grazing in doorways, the closeness of two dishwashers.

He brought what he owned in a small satchel and I cleared out the spare room. On the bed, he deposited an assortment of useless clocks he planned to repair, odd-shaped foreign coins, perfectly kept brushes and paints, a manuscript someone had entrusted to him years ago, dull razor blades, and his three shirts. I charged him no rent and let him eat more or less what he wanted. In return, he filled the corners of my rooms with cuttings he would never plant, destroyed the alphabetical order of my bookshelves, and left the inner workings of his clocks on all the tables. He collected from the street furnishings which he intended for an apartment when he'd saved the money. He carried in a flea-bitten mattress, a picture frame containing someone's grandfather, and a sheepskin coat which he said he could have gotten twenty dollars for on the street but it was my size.

He ate and slept again. His fine, sculpted face soon filled out and got some color in it. I ate less and slept less and talked more. He took me into his confidence and told me he planned to liberate Puerto Rico. He engaged in cryptic conversations and sometimes disappeared in the night. When he left, I didn't inquire. During the phone calls, I went into another room. By day we worked and he took orders from me and never came into my office unless I sent for him and by night he never came into my room.

But sometimes I went into his room. Only at night if I had dreams. Dreams of tidal waves. In some I was a little girl with a bucket. In others, a grown woman traveling on an oceanliner when the sky darkened. Sometimes surfers were riding the waves. If I woke shaking, I went down the corridor and opened his door. I touched his arm and he always made a space for me. One night two silver angels appeared over the bed. They were street angels, rescued from the garbage, and he said they would protect us.

Walking home from the movies, we paused along the river. Staring into the water, José grew nostalgic and began the story of the love affair between his grandparents. His grandfather had been a major like Castro and Ché in what our history books call the Spanish-American War. 'You North Americans get all the credit,' he said. 'We fight for twenty-five years and all anyone remembers is Teddy Roosevelt riding over San Juan Hill.' His grandfather went to New Orleans to raise an army and met another revolutionary, married to a French woman. They had a beautiful daughter who despised the gruff, coarse Cuban, given to belching in public places. She eluded him for three years until her father brought her to Cuba where she met the major again. This time he rode a yellow horse and commanded a batallion. She followed him into the hills.

The moon glistened on the river and I watched it as he spoke because I was distracted. The most exciting member of my family was a great uncle who earned his living by diving from a hundred-foot ladder into the Volga River. I knew of no great loves in my family. My father spent most of his time in a workshop, inventing things. He invented a special glue, a rust-proof metal, and a new lens, and these he patented. My mother worked in another part of the house, designing costumes for her children. In my life I have been a dragon, a money tree, and cotton candy. The night I was a money tree, my friends tore the paper dollars from my branches. I left the party early. It was a night not unlike the night we were walking in and I took the long way because I didn't want my mother to see me upset. The wind blew through my barren branches as I reached the point above the lake where the lovers parked their cars.

It was at that moment, distracted, turned inward, that José put his arm around me and kissed me. Perhaps if he had done so an instant earlier or later, everything would have been different. As it was, it was not a kiss that changes lives or builds empires. When we reached home, we thought of becoming lovers again but the doorbell rang. A young man with an aquiline nose and a star through his left earlobe stood at the door. 'Hello,' I said. 'Can I help you?' He extended his hand.

'I'm a friend of José's,' he said, shaking my hand. 'My name is José.'

The new José, who fortunately was called José Luis, was a journalist en route to Ecuador where he worked for a Marxist press. They had known each other in Cuba and had gone to Puerto Rico together. José Luis was a true communist who lived his beliefs, unlike my husband who was an aristocrat at heart. I gave him the sofa, the only place left.

At times I used to hear them, the rhythmic counterpoint of their foreign words, in the next room. Some of the words reached me. Music, love, revolution. I could hear my own name and then the words drifted back again into the unknown tongue. I wondered if this wasn't the language of all men. Dark, whispered, incomprehensible. I used to hope that inside there, in the next room, they were saying whatever it was that was really important, and yet I was left out of it. I lived in occupied rooms with José and José Luis. Sometimes their voices woke me. One night I tiptoed down the corridor to tell them to be quiet. When I opened the door, I saw José, jaundiced and ugly beneath the somber yellow bulb. They apologized and promised to be quiet and I forgot the whole thing until it happened again.

Even if they didn't stay up talking, sometimes I heard José coughing the deep, rasping cough of an asthmatic. With José Luis there, his work began to drop off. He ate less and was always leaving late at night, going to meetings or to listen to jazz. One night he brought a woman home. She wore a short red skirt and had matted blond hair. He didn't introduce us. When he ordered her to make drinks, she did. She stared at me as if she couldn't decide what I was doing here and I was certain he had found her in the street. When he took her into his room, I did the dishes and clattered the pots and pans. José Luis watched me from the living room and, if he hadn't been there, I probably would have gone into his room and murdered them both. When I woke in the middle of the night, José was sitting on the edge of my bed.

'I've done a terrible thing.' He said he'd only brought her home to punish me for not loving him. I thought of that poor woman and that it wasn't clear he'd loved me. He said someday he wanted to take me to a coffee plantation he knew up in the hills not far from Havana. He ran his hands over the covers, over my nightgown, touching the side of my face, my neck. That day he moved his things into my room and José Luis seemed much happier, now that he could have a room for himself.

One morning over breakfast they told me they were going sailing for a week from Martha's Vineyard to Nova Scotia in the boat of a friend. I remember how they were. Leaning over coffee cups, sunlight cutting a line across the table. I went to the phone and called Lisa. She was my oldest friend from back West. She had been engaged to a man who went to Vietnam but the war had changed him. She came East and lived with my husband and me for a time. In the past year, she had done odd jobs, waitressing, translating from the German, putting commas into manuscripts. I told her two Cubans were living in my apartment and we were going sailing. She said, 'What else is new?' When I asked if she wanted to come along, she said she'd have to think about it. She called back five minutes later and said nothing was keeping her here.

'I'm going with you,' I told them when I returned to the kitchen, 'and I'm bringing a friend.' They raised their eyes at one another. The boat suddenly became smaller. The crew more competent. 'We know how to sail,' I said. We grew up on the Great Lakes. We were once in a dangerous storm. I told them what I knew of the coast of Maine. There were islands that were cemeteries for mussels. Others where crayfish and sand dollars went to die. Still others for turtles, clams, and starfish. I had seen the pictures, miles of desolate beach paved in discarded shells.

On the ferry over, Lisa and José Luis leaned over the railing, staring at the water. A month later she followed him to Peru, then to Ecuador. José and I stood back like proud parents and thought how well-suited they were. The ride was choppy. José Luis, possessing the natural homing instinct of all refugees, had not brought the address of the people who owned the boat. Rum, he said, would help. On the island we sat below a statue

of a whale and proceeded in a methodical way to get drunk.
José patted the whale. 'In the old city of San Juan,' he said,
'there is a statue of Ponce de Leon. The finger on his right hand
points to the south and I can't tell you how many nights I sat
drunk in that square, waiting for the finger to move.'

'What's south?' I asked, expecting to hear Cuba. The rum had
ruined my sense of geography.

'The Atlantic Ocean,' he said. We found the North Star and
told tales of failed navigators. Columbus, for instance, had been
looking for India. Once I found a bald eagle a thousand miles
off course, sitting in a tree. Lisa remembered. José Luis turned
his head like a beacon, trying to recall the road which eluded
us. We found a beach. José said the eagle was probably just
curious. Lisa yawned. We drank like fraternity brothers. Somewhere far away Barbara Walters was interviewing Fidel Castro.

'Do you live in a house?' Barbara asked.

'I even sleep in a bed,' Fidel replied.

While we slept, José was in town, being arrested on charges
of drunken, disorderly conduct, the theft of a bicycle, and lighting firecrackers. The owner of the bicycle dropped the charges
when it was returned but insisted José be deported. We found
him toward dusk when we went to the police station to report
him missing. José Luis said this always happened when no one
needed it. He took Lisa to the house of his friends with the boat,
which he finally recalled was a mile up the road from the
station. José was behind bars and asked me for a dime which
he used to call a lawyer he didn't have from a phone that didn't
exist. He said he'd been interrogated under lights, tortured with
objects on his wrists, denied his civil rights, but he hadn't
divulged the holdout of the revolutionary forces which he confided in me because he saw I could be trusted; he whispered in
my ear my own address. When the guard pointed to his head,
indicating José was crazy, José pleaded with the guard not to
shoot himself.

I told the guard to keep him until he came to his senses and
the guard said he had not intended to do anything else. He told

me José thought he was being tortured when they booked him and had tried to eat a bar of soap. As I was leaving, José called me back. 'When the finger moves, we move.'

'You're drunk,' I said. 'Get some sleep.'

He nodded, agreeing with me. Then in a moment of unique lucidity he added, 'We left Cuba in an airplane. Not a raft.' He dropped back onto his cot. 'American Airlines to be specific.'

I began climbing the mile-long hill which led to the house where we'd stay. It was a steep hill and I climbed slowly. Somewhere at sea our boat was anchored and José still didn't suspect that I didn't know a bow from a mainsail. But then he'd invented a raft of cocoanut shells. I climbed, legs stiff and weary from a bad night's sleep on the beach. Sea breezes blew through the pines. Somber, spectral trees. I was tired and it came to me slowly and went slowly like waves. It came to me, then went away as in a dream, a dream growing and rising at its own pace, the way anything can come when you climb a hill on a clear night.

The guard opened the door, sleepy-eyed. 'It's not morning, yet.' He was buttoning his shirt.

'I forgot to tell him something,' I said. I stood there wondering why women with brains and good jobs will relinquish it all for a pair of arms, a night companion. And then how they will confuse that for love.

'Five minutes.' The guard stepped back and unlocked the door that led to the cells. In one of the cells a drunk was singing 'America, The Beautiful.' José lay, crumpled, mouth open, sleeping. Though only eight years younger than myself, he looked innocent as a baby. I tapped on the bars. Then I banged on them. The drunk winced. Finally José opened one eye, then the other. He looked at me, groaned, and tried to get up, but lay back. At that moment I wanted to go to jail too. I wanted to be locked up, put away. I wanted to do something bad, something dangerous. I pounded on the bars now.

'You're gonna wake the dead,' the guard said. 'Or at least the sheriff.' I didn't know if Martha's Vineyard had a sheriff but I was prepared to wake him. I clung to the bars like a monkey until José, seeing that I wasn't going away, stumbled from his cot over to the bars.

He wrapped his arms around my neck and tried to kiss me through the bars. My jaw bones hit metal.

'Do you love me?' He stared at me, not sure of what I meant.

'I care about you,' he replied solemnly. We were whispering and the drunk leaned forward trying to hear. The guard had already given up on us and went back to his cot in the next room. He was touching my face.

'Well, after we go on the boat to Nova Scotia,' I said, 'I want you to leave; I think it would be better.'

He nodded. 'I was planning to leave anyway as soon as we got back.'

'What do you mean, you were planning to leave?' I was trembling. How could he plan to leave? Hadn't I given him a home, food, and more? My body shook and I could not contain myself. I wanted him to beg me to let him stay; after all I'd done for him, how could he want to leave me? The illogic of it all escaped me but I felt the tears well in my eyes and for the first time in years I felt as I had the night I wore the costume of a money tree.

'Time's up, lady,' the guard yelled.

'Look,' José said, 'I'll see you in the morning, all right?' He patted me on the cheek. 'We'll work it all out tomorrow.' Then he fell back on his cot and was asleep.

The guard escorted me to the door. 'Don't worry, lady, I'll take good care of him. I've got children of my own.'

José left for Nazaré after he finished the Spanish Harlem series and sent me a postcard, the same one I had on my wall, but with his thin form scribbled in the sand. I wandered a maze of rooms, perceiving things that weren't there. A ratty mattress, the sun carving a table top, foreign words floating down corridors like refugees on their rafts. Lisa, back from Ecuador after a tumult with José Luis, stayed with me. She lost her job for refusing to put commas into manuscripts, saying that they were just one more repetition. The semicolon became her only trusted punctuation, the pause to reflect, then move on.

In pictures from the journey, I am like this. Caught in a sail, holding a fish. But mostly when I think about it, it is this way. It is something barely visible, hardly seen. Usually it is walking up a hill, content with the elementary things. Wind through branches, solitary laughter, moonlight on water like coins in a beggar's cup. When I married the criminal attorney who solved the Nicholson murder, José was on the masthead at Disney Studios. This marriage endures. He is American and we travel a lot.

FOR THE BEST IN PAPERBACKS, LOOK FOR THE

In every corner of the world, on every subject under the sun, Penguin represents quality and variety—the very best in publishing today.

For complete information about books available from Penguin—including Pelicans, Puffins, Peregrines, and Penguin Classics—and how to order them, write to us at the appropriate address below. Please note that for copyright reasons the selection of books varies from country to country.

In the United Kingdom: For a complete list of books available from Penguin in the U.K., please write to *Dept E.P., Penguin Books Ltd, Harmondsworth, Middlesex, UB7 0DA*.

In the United States: For a complete list of books available from Penguin in the U.S., please write to *Dept BA, Penguin,* Box 120, Bergenfield, New Jersey 07621-0120.

In Canada: For a complete list of books available from Penguin in Canada, please write to *Penguin Books Ltd, 2801 John Street, Markham, Ontario L3R 1B4*.

In Australia: For a complete list of books available from Penguin in Australia, please write to the *Marketing Department, Penguin Books Ltd, P.O. Box 257, Ringwood, Victoria 3134*.

In New Zealand: For a complete list of books available from Penguin in New Zealand, please write to the *Marketing Department, Penguin Books (NZ) Ltd, Private Bag, Takapuna, Auckland 9*.

In India: For a complete list of books available from Penguin, please write to *Penguin Overseas Ltd, 706 Eros Apartments, 56 Nehru Place, New Delhi, 110019*.

In Holland: For a complete list of books available from Penguin in Holland, please write to *Penguin Books Nederland B.V., Postbus 195, NL-1380AD Weesp, Netherlands*.

In Germany: For a complete list of books available from Penguin, please write to *Penguin Books Ltd, Friedrichstrasse 10-12, D-6000 Frankfurt Main I, Federal Republic of Germany*.

In Spain: For a complete list of books available from Penguin in Spain, please write to *Longman, Penguin España, Calle San Nicolas 15, E-28013 Madrid, Spain*.

In Japan: For a complete list of books available from Penguin in Japan, please write to *Longman Penguin Japan Co Ltd, Yamaguchi Building, 2-12-9 Kanda Jimbocho, Chiyoda-Ku, Tokyo 101, Japan*.